What is Indiana Jones doing in Egypt in May 1908?

He's on a worldwide tour with his parents. He's stuck with a pesky tutor. And he's a little bit bored—until he meets a mummy!

He's introduced to it by some of the biggest names in archaeology, who've led him to a just-discovered tomb . . . soon to be the scene of murder!

Watch Indy explore the past, jump into mystery . . . and blaze a trail to lifelong adventure!

Catch the whole story of Young Indy's travels on the amazing fact-and-fiction television series *The Young Indiana Jones Chronicles!*

THE YOUNG INDIANA JONES CHRONICLES
(novels based on the television series)

YOUNG INDIANA JONES BOOKS
(original novels)

Young Indiana Jones and the . . .

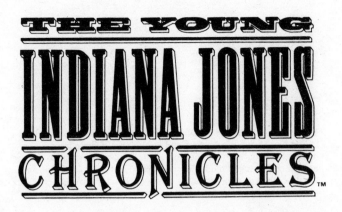

The Mummy's Curse

Adapted by Megan Stine and H. William Stine

Based on the "Egypt, May 1908" segment of
the television film *The Curse of the Jackal*

Teleplay by Jonathan Hales

Story by George Lucas

Directed by Jim O'Brien

With photographs from the film

RANDOM HOUSE 🏠 NEW YORK

This is a work of fiction. While Young Indiana Jones is portrayed as
taking part in historical events and meeting real figures from history,
many of the characters in the story as well as the situations and scenes
have been invented. In addition, where real historical figures and events
are described, in some cases the chronology and historical facts have
been altered for dramatic effect.

Copyright © 1992 by Lucasfilm Ltd. (LFL)
All rights reserved under International and Pan-American Copyright
Conventions. Published in the United States by Random House, Inc.,
New York, and simultaneously in Canada by Random House of Canada
Limited, Toronto.

PHOTO CREDITS: Cover photograph by Craig Blankenhorn, © 1991 by
Capital Cities/ABC. Interior photographs by Craig Blankenhorn (1, 5, 6,
9), © 1991 by Capital Cities/ABC; and Keith Hamshere (2, 3, 4, 7, 8, 10),
© 1992 by Lucasfilm Ltd. Map by Alfred Giuliani.

Library of Congress Cataloging-in-Publication Data
Stine, Megan.
    The mummy's curse / adapted by Megan Stine, H. William Stine ;
teleplay by Jonathan Hales ; story by George Lucas; directed by Jim
O'Brien.
        p.   cm. — (Young Indiana Jones Chronicles ; TV-1)
    "Based on the 'Egypt, May 1908' segment of the television film *The
Curse of the Jackal,* with photographs from the film." Includes
bibliographical references (p.).
    Summary: In Egypt in 1908, nine-year-old Indiana Jones meets
Lawrence of Arabia and encounters a mystery involving a mummy's
curse and a murdered guard at an archeological dig.
    ISBN 0-679-82774-9 (pbk.)
    [1. Mummies—Fiction. 2. Egypt—Fiction. 3. Lawrence, T. E.
(Thomas Edward), 1888–1935—Fiction. 4. Mystery and detective
stories.] I. Stine, H. William. II. Hales, Jonathan. III. Lucas,
George . IV. Curse of the jackal. V. Title. VI. Series.
PZ7.S86035Ms 1992 [Fic]—dc20   91-53167

Manufactured in the United States of America   10 9 8 7 6 5 4 3 2 1

The Mummy's Curse

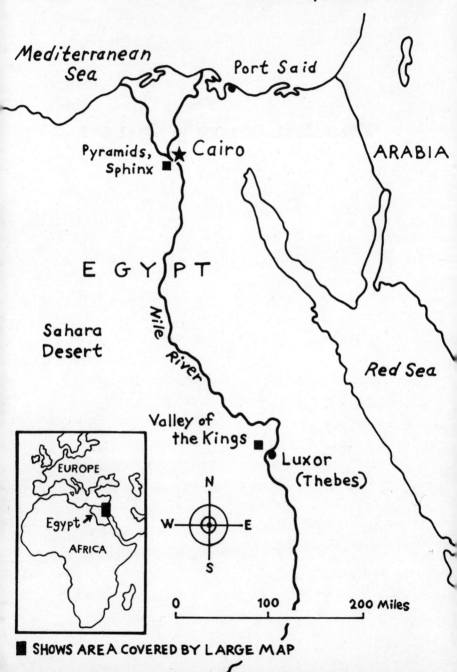

INDY'S TERRITORY IN "EGYPT, MAY 1908"

Mediterranean
Sea

Port Said

Pyramids,
Sphinx

★ Cairo

ARABIA

E G Y P T

Nile River

Sahara
Desert

Red Sea

Valley of
the Kings

Luxor
(Thebes)

EUROPE

Egypt

AFRICA

N

W   E

S

0   100   200 Miles

■ SHOWS AREA COVERED BY LARGE MAP

Chapter 1

"Yanks, are ya?" asked the cabdriver, turning around to look at young Indiana Jones.

Indy sat between his mother and father in an open horse-drawn carriage that clattered over uneven cobblestone streets. He was getting his first look at the city of Oxford, England. The sky was gray, the May air wet and cool.

"Yanks?" asked young Indy, looking up at the cabdriver, who was perched on a seat above.

"He means, are we American?" Indy's father explained.

"Oh. You bet," Indy said cheerfully. "At least

3

I am. My father was born in Scotland, but I guess he's American now. He's a professor at Princeton University in New Jersey."

"A professor—I'm not surprised," said the driver. "There's more professors in this city than I can shake my whip at. Some days it's 'ard not running over a dozen of them." He laughed, then clicked his tongue to urge the trotting horse on.

Indy leaned forward to watch the scene that was passing in front of him.

Beautiful spires towered over his head. University scholars dressed in flowing black robes filled the streets. Statues and monuments were everywhere. The carriage passed one particularly gruesome collection of stone heads that looked to Indy as if they had been chopped off and then placed on columns eight feet high.

"You know, Junior," Professor Henry Jones said, breaking the silence, "Oxford is a very old city. The university here was founded in 1163, when Henry the Second was King of England."

" 'Ee's a professor, all right," said the cab-driver with a laugh.

Indiana sighed. Yes, his father was a smart man, a very smart man. He was a professor of medieval literature. He spent all his time reading, and when he wasn't reading, he was teaching people what he had read.

But if he's so smart, Indy thought to himself, why can't he ever remember that I *hate* being called Junior? Or Henry. Why did they have to name me Henry Jones, Jr.? I want to be called Indiana! So what if my dog has the same name!

"Stop the cab!" Professor Jones suddenly called. "This is it! This is the house."

The driver brought the carriage to a quick stop in front of a small two-story brick house with a tiny garden in front.

Indy jumped out of the cab while his father helped his mother out.

"You know, Anna," Professor Jones said to his wife, "I haven't set foot here since the day I graduated from university." He straightened his brown tweed suit and gave his thin beard and mustache a quick swipe with his hand to comb them. "That was fifteen years ago—class of 1893. You're going to meet a great teacher here, Junior. And she's going to be a wonderful tutor for you."

Indy stopped dead in his tracks. "A *what?*"

"A tutor," said Professor Jones, leading the way to the front door. "I've asked Miss Seymour to join us on my lecture tour. Didn't I tell you, Junior?"

"No," Indy said, still not moving from the sidewalk. "You said we were coming here to

5

meet one of *your* old tutors."

"Must have slipped my mind somehow," Professor Jones said.

"Henry, dear," said Indy's mother. Everything about her was soft and understanding, including her touch, her voice, the gaze of her blue eyes, and her smile. "You haven't even met Miss Seymour yet."

Professor Jones knocked on the front door, which was soon opened by a young woman in a long black maid's uniform. She showed them into a small study with an unlighted fireplace and asked them to wait.

Stepping into that dark room felt to Indy like walking into a prison or a cave. The room seemed even smaller because it was lined, ceiling to floor, with shelves of books.

While his father walked about examining the volumes, Indy's mother sat calmly in a leather chair. Indy sat beside her, tapping his foot nervously and pulling at his bow tie.

"Don't fidget, Junior," said his father.

"I'm not fidgeting. I'm squirming."

"And don't be fresh in front of your mother."

Suddenly the door to the room opened. In walked a tall, rigidly straight woman in her sixties, her gray hair pulled back tight. Her starched white blouse and black skirt crinkled and creaked as she walked. Or maybe that was *her* creaking.

"Mr. Jones," said the woman warmly, holding out her hand. *"Professor* Jones, I should say. What a pleasure to see you again!"

Indy blinked. She acted as if she and his father were old friends. As if she had seen him last week—instead of fifteen years ago.

"Miss Seymour," said Professor Henry Jones, "I would like you to meet my wife, Anna. And my son, Henry Jones, Jr." He smiled at Indy. "Junior, this is your new tutor, Miss Helen Seymour."

That's a tutor? Indy said to himself. Holy smokes!

"Remember your manners, Henry," Indy's mother said.

Indy shook hands with Miss Seymour, but he pulled his hand back as soon as he could.

Miss Seymour stared at Indy silently for a moment. Then she spoke to his father, her eyes still glued to young Indiana Jones. "His clothes are appalling and his posture leaves much to be desired."

Great! Indy thought. She doesn't want anything to do with me!

"Henry, dear," said Indy's mother, "stand up straight."

With everyone telling him what to do, Indy felt even more like a prisoner. He glanced out the window at the gloomy gray clouds and then over at his mother. Her blue dress suit looked like a lost piece of sky in the dark room. Finally he lifted his head to stare Miss Seymour directly in the eye.

"Young man," said Miss Seymour. "How old are you?" She pronounced each word clearly and loudly, and her proper British accent sounded harsh compared with Indy's father's light Scottish brogue.

I can tell just by looking at her that she hates me, Indy thought. He swallowed hard and tried to remember what she had just said.

"Are you deaf?" Miss Seymour demanded.

"Nine," Indy said. But he had to clear his throat twice before the word would come out.

"And he mumbles," Miss Seymour told Professor Jones with disapproval.

"Nine. I am nine years old," said Indy, pronouncing each word clearly and loudly.

"And are you anxious to learn?" she said, taking a couple of quick steps toward him.

"It depends," Indy said.

"It depends?" she repeated. "It depends on what?"

"On what's being taught," Indy said, cocking

his head and giving her a sly smile.

Miss Seymour frowned. "I'm sorry," she said, turning to Indy's father. "It's impossible. It's quite impossible. The boy is far too young. My pupils are university students. I have never taught anyone so young. In fact, I have never before *spoken* to anyone so young."

"Anna," said the professor to his wife, "would you take Junior out of the room for a moment, please?"

Indy didn't need to be told twice to leave. He was glad to get out of there as fast as he could. "I hate her. She's a witch," he complained to his mother as soon as they were in the hall. " 'Tutor' is probably the way British people say 'torture.' She'll ruin our whole trip!"

Indy's mother smiled. With a soft hand, she tried to push Indy's brown hair back from his forehead. But everything about Indiana Jones defied control. "Henry," said Anna Jones, "Miss Seymour must be a wonderful teacher. She tutored your father when he went to the university here."

"Then let *him* study with her!" Indy said.

Inside the library, Indy's father was mounting a campaign of persuasion on Miss Seymour. He pretended to thumb a book as he spoke. "If I remember correctly from our conversations when I was a student, Miss Seymour, you have always wanted to travel. And this is your chance—the chance of a lifetime."

"Yes, it is," she admitted, "but I won't go a single mile with *that* boy."

"Not even to see the Great Wall of China? The gardens of Kyoto? The Taj Mahal by moonlight? Sunset over the pyramids?" He held these treats out to her as if offering chocolates to a small child.

"Will you really go to all of those places, Professor Jones?"

"Miss Seymour," he said, "as I wrote you, I am embarking on a two-year lecture tour of universities around the world. I am speaking on the medieval chivalric code and the Holy Grail, topics of great importance to me. The tour will take me to all of those wonderful places, and more. My family must go wherever I go—but my son *cannot* go without a teacher, a splendid teacher. Someone like you."

"Your son doesn't need a teacher," said Miss Seymour. "He needs a governess. Someone to teach him manners and posture and elocution! And considering the boy's attitude, you might even need a jailer!"

"There are times, Miss Seymour, when I totally agree with you," Professor Jones said, chuckling lightly. "But think about it. . . . When will you ever again have an opportunity like this? *When?*"

Miss Seymour looked at him with a pained expression that slowly changed to one of yearning . . . deep yearning . . .

Outside in the hallway, Indy sat in an uncomfortable, tall-backed chair, hoping that Miss Seymour would stick to her guns and refuse to take the job. Don't come with us, he prayed. Just don't.

"Mr. Jones?" said Miss Seymour.

The voice startled him. He hadn't heard the door to the small study swing open.

"Stand up straight and be alert!" Miss Seymour said. "I don't allow my students to daydream."

"Y-your students?" Indy stammered, rising to his feet.

"Yes, Mr. Jones. For the next two years I am going to be your tutor."

Indy sat down quickly. Two years of reading, studying, doing homework, taking tests under the glare of Miss Seymour's steely blue eyes? Two whole years?

Holy smokes! Indy thought. I'll never last that long!

Chapter 2

Ten days later, Indy found himself aboard an ocean liner bound for Cairo, Egypt. In the small, sweltering cabin, the only sounds were the hissing of gas lamps, the turning of pages in the books Indy and Miss Seymour were studying, and the creaking of the ship as it pitched and heaved across the waves.

Outside the cabin, the wind howled and gigantic waves crashed over the decks. For three straight days the wind had fought the ship for every sailing mile. Now, as the ocean liner moved into the Bay of Biscay, the storm seemed to be winning the battle.

"That must be a whale of a storm out there," Indy said wistfully. What he really meant was that he wanted to run up on deck to feel the salt spray in his face and try to stand against the rolling of the ocean liner.

Miss Seymour looked up from her book. She did not appear to be pleased by the interruption. "Mr. Jones, if you are distracted by a little choppy sailing weather, then I see I have not challenged your concentration adequately. Instead of reading to page forty, please read to page eighty."

Indy slumped in his chair. Not because he wanted to, but because the ship suddenly rolled as it met a new wave.

"Posture, Mr. Jones. Posture," said Miss Seymour.

She didn't seem to notice that there was a huge storm all around them. Or that all of the books and notebooks, along with the map, slate, and globe, were occasionally sliding from one side of the cramped cabin to the other.

"Egypt, Mr. Jones, is a truly remarkable country," Miss Seymour said. She closed her book and rubbed her eyes. "Its history can be traced back to 3000 B.C."

You probably knew lots of people back then,

Indy said to himself.

The ship unexpectedly jumped and a shelf of books went crashing to the floor. Miss Seymour lurched forward awkwardly on the rolling floor to pick them up. Indy secretly laughed.

"Will we climb the Great Pyramid in Egypt, Miss Seymour?"

"Climb the pyramids?" she repeated, as if she couldn't believe his question.

Indy could guess what that meant. "I was just asking," he said. He felt his hopes for any adventure on this trip about to sink under the crashing waves. "I guess we'll probably just study pictures of them in books."

"Young Mr. Jones," said Miss Seymour, standing as straight as she could under the stormy conditions, "I have not lived this long nor come this far to deny myself the joy of feeling antiquity beneath my feet. Oh, yes, Mr. Jones, we shall climb the pyramids—and we shall stand on the top, closer to heaven than we have ever stood." Her eyes seemed to grow misty as she spoke.

"Golly, thanks, Miss Seymour!" Indy said, eyeing her with new appreciation. Maybe she wasn't such an old witch after all. Indy was so excited he could hardly sit still. Climbing a pyramid—now *that* was his idea of a course of study! "But Miss Seymour, how can we stand on the top of a pyramid? Doesn't it come to a point at the top?"

The look of happiness faded from her face. She snatched up a book and flipped through its pages until she found the one she wanted.

"Don't they teach you anything in the American colonies, Mr. Jones? Read immediately to page one hundred and twenty-three."

"That'll take all night!" Indy moaned.

As it turned out, it didn't take all night. It only took all day. Indy finally left his tutor's cabin when it was time to dress for dinner.

And even then he still found himself under the watchful eye of Miss Seymour. Indy, his mother and father, and Miss Seymour all sat at the captain's table every night for dinner. Also at the table were three other British passengers: Mr. and Mrs. Smythe, a middle-aged couple, and Bishop Dollope, an aging and thin man. The bishop reminded Indy a lot of a tall, leafy plant that hadn't been watered for a dangerously long time.

After a few days of eating with the other passengers, Indy had begun to understand Miss Seymour better. He realized that she wasn't being strange—she was simply being British. No matter how rough the seas were, the British acted as though it were just an inconvenience and nothing dangerous. They never showed any emotion. Indy really wanted to do something to shake them up.

"Good evening, everyone. Heavy weather, Captain," said the bishop on this particularly turbulent night. The last to join the party, he stumbled as the ship rolled, and grabbed the back of his chair to steady himself.

"A bit lively, Bishop," said the captain, catching his wineglass before it tipped with the ship's motion. "I hope it's not spoiling your enjoyment of the voyage."

"Oh, no. Not at all," the bishop said, sitting down. He smiled a greeting to Miss Seymour. "We British are a hardy island breed, what? Salty dogs and all that."

Indy looked around the dining room with its many round tables draped with white linen cloths. Each table was set with sparkling china and gleaming silverware. But although the ship's passenger lists were full, the dining room was quite empty. Most of the passengers were too seasick to show any interest in food.

"Well, young fellow," said the captain, looking at Indy. Somehow his voice never seemed to leave his nose. "How are your studies progressing?"

"Fine, thank you, sir," Indy answered politely. At least she hasn't put leg irons on me yet, he thought to himself.

"Capital!" the captain exclaimed, beaming at Indy's father and mother and then at Miss Seymour. "And what did you learn today?"

"I learned that most pyramids are flat at the top and not pointed," Indy said. "That's because the top has usually been worn away."

"Well done, lad," the captain said. "There is nothing more satisfying than to see a boy enjoying the fruits of his studies."

"Thank you, sir," Indy said politely. If he had to say "thank you, sir" one more time he knew he'd politely go out of his mind. "I also learned about mummies," Indy added.

"Mummies?" said the captain.

"Yes, sir. I learned about how the ancient Egyptians turned people into mummies when they died."

"Junior," said Professor Jones.

Indy heard the warning in his father's voice, but he ignored it.

"Really?" the captain said, looking quite interested. "I say. And how did they go about that?"

"Well," Indy began, enjoying himself on the voyage for the first time. "First, they waited a few days, sir. They needed the body soft, you see. Then they scooped out the brain."

Mrs. Smythe choked and even Indy's mother put down her spoon. But the captain was still listening, so Indy quickly continued.

"Yeah, they took the brain out through the nose. Of course, they had to break it first . . . right here." Indy pointed to the strip of cartilage separating his nostrils. "They used a metal hook," he said, picking up his fork, "and sort of teased it out."

"Excuse me," said Mrs. Smythe, standing quickly and leaving the table as fast as she could.

Indy wondered if he could actually make a clean sweep of the table. This was his idea of fun!

"Then they took a stone knife," Indy continued, lifting his dinner knife, "and cut open the left side of the corpse, and reached in and pulled out the lower organs. All except the kidneys, that is. Then they cut the chest open." He drew a straight line on the tablecloth with his knife. "They hauled out everything except the heart. They washed all the organs in salt, then poured hot goo over them and wrapped them up. Like gift wrapping, I guess."

Mr. Smythe rose shakily to his feet.

"I think I'd better check on my wife," he said. He looked as if he were going to throw up in ten seconds. And unfortunately he was twenty seconds away from the nearest bathroom. He bolted across the dining room for the door.

Got another one, Indy thought gleefully.

"Then they put the four organs—the liver, the lungs, the stomach, and the intestines—in separate jars," Indy went on. Out of the corner of his eye, he saw his mother scoot her chair back and leave. "After that, they cleaned out the body with palm wine and spices; then they dried it off with salt and sawdust and stuff. They tied on the toenails and fingernails with string so they wouldn't fall off." He turned to the bishop and said, "Wasn't that considerate?"

Bishop Dollope looked at his food with revulsion. Then he glared coldly at Miss Seymour and left the table.

Now there were only Indy, his father, the captain, and Miss Seymour remaining. Indy turned his attention to Miss Seymour. She was the one he wanted to get to the most.

"They packed the body with rags soaked in oils and then sewed it up again. And they plugged up the nose and stuck bits of cloth under the eyelids. Although, you know what I read—and this is the real interesting part, Miss

19

Seymour—sometimes, they used little onions instead!"

Pow! That got her. Miss Seymour put down her fork and left.

"Of course," Indy said to the captain, "that completed just the first stage—the embalming. Then they had to wrap the whole body in bandages. It didn't always work, though. Most often the mummies *leaked.*"

The captain stood up so quickly that he knocked his chair over behind him. "I believe I'm wanted on the bridge," he said, before making a speedy exit.

"That was an interesting speech, Junior," said Professor Jones.

"Thank you, Father," Indy said, trying very hard not to laugh.

"Very thorough and very graphic," Professor Jones said.

"Miss Seymour is an excellent tutor, Father," Indy gushed insincerely.

"Now finish your dinner. Eat your tripe," said Professor Jones, as he pulled a book out of his pocket. "You *do* know what tripe is, don't you?"

Indiana Jones gave his father a quizzical look.

"Stomach," Professor Jones said. "The muscular lining of an ox's stomach, to be precise."

Stomach! With a jerk of his head, Indiana

looked down at his dinner. Suddenly every-thing on his plate was swimming around. Indy's own stomach did a quick, sickening somersault, warning him that it was about to do much worse—very soon.

He jumped out of his chair and careened out of the dining room. All the way he could hear his father chuckling behind him.

Chapter 3

"I'm off," Indy told his parents as soon as their bags were unloaded in their hotel rooms.

Outside the windows of their second-floor suite, the city of Cairo bustled and steamed. Strange voices and mysterious smells beckoned to Indy. After so many days of seeing nothing but water and Miss Seymour, Indy finally had solid ground under his feet and new sights to explore.

Together, he and Miss Seymour ventured out to investigate the winding streets and alleyways of Cairo. When they reached the crowded street market, merchants instantly surrounded them. Some waved gold bracelets and jeweled rings. Others held handwoven rugs, pottery, knives, live chickens and dead ones in front of their faces, begging them to buy.

Then Indy stared transfixed for a long while, watching a thin man who wore only a cloth around his head and a cloth around his waist. The man played an eerie-sounding horn that seemed to hypnotize a five-foot cobra. It was the longest snake Indy had ever seen. Its head even with Indy's, the deadly snake swayed and swooped, as if following the rhythm of the snake charmer's music.

Everything in Egypt was different and exciting, and Indy loved it. From now on, he decided, he always wanted his life to be filled with new adventures. He promised himself he'd never do the same thing twice as long as he lived.

In the following days, Professor Jones began his lectures at the university. Anna Jones attended tea parties and other social functions. Indy and Miss Seymour settled down to lessons, with time out for lots of sight-seeing.

One morning Indy's mother informed him that she and the professor were leaving Cairo for the weekend. A British diplomat had invited them to a house party. "Will you and Miss Seymour be able to keep busy, Henry dear?" she asked.

"No problem," Indy said. Keep busy? he thought. How could he help but keep busy, with all of Egypt before him!

Late on Saturday afternoon, Indy and Miss Seymour boosted themselves up into the saddles of two camels. It was their first camel ride! Then they headed west, out of Cairo and into the desert.

Their guide was a toothless old camel driver who didn't speak a word of English. Occasionally he'd look over at Indy, who was struggling to keep his balance as the camel walked. Each time the guide looked, he laughed and said something in Arabic. To Indy, the language sounded like talking backward. Meanwhile, Miss Seymour looked perfectly comfortable on her camel. She wasn't wobbling at all. How does she do it? Indy wondered.

As the ride went on, Indy was surprised to see the landscape change dramatically. The land near Cairo had been green and fertile, fed by the waters of the Nile River. Now, however, as they moved west, waves of heat danced above the sand. There was nothing on the horizon, except for an isolated palm tree here and there.

It was as if they had crossed an imaginary line on an imaginary map . . . moving from green to brown.

In the desert, Indy learned how to adjust to the slow, awkward movements of his camel. And he liked sitting so high above the ground. The only thing he *couldn't* get used to was the camel's smell.

Finally, when they had been riding for more than two hours, the guide pointed off into the distance and shouted.

There, where he was pointing, Indy saw three triangular structures silhouetted against the empty desert. This is it, Indy thought. These were the tombs of ancient kings, the last resting places of the souls of the pharaohs: the pyramids.

The tallest one was called the Great Pyramid of Cheops. But Indy knew from his studies that Cheops was not the correct name for the Egyptian king, or pharaoh, who had built this tomb. Cheops was the Greek name. The Egyptian name was Khufu.

Suddenly the facts Indy had memorized took on real meaning. Silently he recited what he'd learned. That the Great Pyramid was an enormous four-sided monument of almost perfect dimensions, nearly five hundred feet tall. That it had been built more than four thousand years ago, as a tomb for just one person, Khufu. That it contained secret doors and passageways leading to the burial chamber where the mummy of Khufu had been laid to rest. And, most amazing of all, that at one time the pyramid was filled with all kinds of treasure—precious objects, furniture, clothing, and jewelry buried with Khufu to keep him happy in his life after death.

The Great Pyramid stood beside two smaller pyramids that were also tombs. But beyond it was the most amazing thing Indy had ever seen in his life. A strange, enormous sculpture six stories tall sat in stately repose. Its body was that of a lion, but it had the head of a man. "The Sphinx," Indy said through his slightly parched lips.

To Indy, the Sphinx was even more mysterious than the pyramids. No one knew for sure when or why it had been built. But according to Miss Seymour, it had very likely been built at the same time as the pyramids—"to guard the entrance to the Nile valley," she said. In another part of Egypt, there were more sphinxes—a whole row of them, in fact. Indy thought it would be wonderful to see them one day.

On the driver's command, the camels stopped

and knelt in the sand, and Indy jumped from his animal's back. The giant structures loomed over him. Indy had never felt so small in his life. He took a big gulp of water from his canteen. He felt dirty and gritty, at the very edge of the world. And he loved it.

The Sphinx seemed to stare down, demanding to know why strangers had come to disturb the pharaoh's sleep. Indy stared back, but his staring match was interrupted by the sound of angry shouting. Indy looked around to see the guide yelling incomprehensibly at Miss Seymour.

"What's wrong?" he asked.

"He keeps trying to hand back the ten piastres I gave him for bringing us here," Miss Seymour said.

"Ten piastres?" said Indy. "But our interpreter said the fee was thirty."

"These people expect to barter. It is part of their nature. You will see: By the time we are finished climbing the pyramid, he will be perfectly content," Miss Seymour insisted.

Indy looked at the man, who kept shouting furiously in Arabic and slapping one hand on the other, demanding more money.

"I don't know, Miss Seymour," Indy said. "He sounds pretty mad to me. Maybe you shouldn't argue with this guy in the middle of the desert."

"Nonsense, Mr. Jones." She cut him off in that tone of voice teachers always used when they expected to have the last word. "Time is passing. Let's get on." With that she turned her back on the camel driver and led Indy across the sand to the Great Pyramid. They stood so close that they could barely see the top. Then they moved on and began to climb one of the smaller pyramids that rose nearby. Grasping the sides of the stones, they lifted themselves up, foot by foot, block by block.

"Did you expect that something this old could be this beautiful?" Miss Seymour asked.

Indy shook his head. "Why can't we climb the biggest pyramid, Miss Seymour?"

"I shall be happy to reach the top of *this* one, Mr. Jones. Do you know when the Great Pyramid was built?"

Of course Indy knew. He not only knew how old it was, but he also knew which dynasty King Khufu had been part of (the fourth), what the stone blocks were made of (sandstone and limestone), and why there were so many stones missing (they had been stolen by ancient builders to make bridges and other buildings). Indy recited all of this for Miss Seymour's benefit.

"Very impressive, " she said, eyeing him with approval.

The one thing Indy didn't know was how the ancient Egyptians had managed to move so many heavy blocks. Each one weighed at least two and a half tons. The mystery of how the pyramids had been built was something even Miss Seymour couldn't answer. Nobody knew for sure.

It took Indy and Miss Seymour nearly until sunset to reach the summit of the pyramid. And then, with the sun burning red in the final minutes of the day, they stood looking down at the endless desert around them.

"This is a sight worth waiting your entire life to see," Miss Seymour said.

"I guess King Khufu was pretty old by the time they finally finished the Great Pyramid," said Indy.

"Some pharaohs lived to a great age. Rameses the Second was over ninety when he died."

I'll bet he had to be *carried* up here at that age, Indy thought to himself.

"Others were mere boys, not much older than you, Mr. Jones," said Miss Seymour.

"It must have been great to be a pharaoh," Indy said wistfully.

"If you look at the shape of the pyramid, you

can see why some people thought it symbol-
ized the rays of the sun descending to
earth . . ."

But Indy wasn't listening anymore. Miss Seymour's voice drifted off with the wind as he began to imagine what it would have been like to
be a pharaoh.

He saw himself standing on top of the Great
Pyramid, dressed in white robes trimmed with
real gold, wearing the king's crown. He was
holding the sacred crook and flail—a long staff
and a small whip—across his chest, just like the
pharaohs in the books he had read. Below him,
tens of thousands of men and women looked
up in awe at their pharaoh—Pharaoh Indiana.
Thousands of soldiers—archers in war chariots
and foot soldiers with shields and battleaxes—
lifted their golden weapons and saluted him with
a mighty cheer. But he was so high above them,
it sounded like a mere whisper. Pharaoh Indiana lifted his arms to the sky and then pointed
down, down to where his subjects stood prepared to die for him.

But one of his subjects seemed to be leaving.
Indy snapped out of his daydream. He pointed
toward the ground. "Look, Miss Seymour! The
camel driver is riding away!"

"Oh my goodness—and he's taking *our*

camels!" Miss Seymour cried.

Indy immediately started scrambling down the pyramid as fast as he could. "Hey, wait!" he yelled to the camel driver. "Don't leave us!"

But Indy knew it was no use. The rat had deliberately waited until they were at the top of the pyramid and then taken off. It was his way of letting Miss Seymour know that he was *not* happy about the ten piastres. Indy's feet slipped on the crumbling surface of the pyramid. When he grabbed to hold on, the sandstone edges cut into his hands.

Finally he reached the bottom, breathing hard and soaking in his own sweat. But all he could do was watch helplessly as the camel driver, the camels, and the canteens and supplies disappeared over the sand.

Twenty minutes later Miss Seymour arrived at the base and stumbled onto the sand, unsteady on her old legs, exhausted.

"Oh, dear," she said quietly.

"I guess he wasn't perfectly content after all," Indy said innocently. "Now we'll have to walk back."

"Walk back? To Cairo?" said Miss Seymour. "Oh, no. We'd never—"

She didn't finish her sentence, but Indy could fill in the missing words. They'd never make it.

They were stuck out in the middle of the desert—alone. Suddenly everything looked different. Spookier, somehow.

Miss Seymour saw the look on Indy's face and cleared her throat. "What I meant was it would be foolish for us to start now because it will be dark soon."

That was true. The yellow desert was turning gray. And as the sun dipped lower, the shadows of the pyramids lengthened and darkened on the sand. Indy watched them cautiously. They seemed to be moving slowly toward him, reaching out to grab him.

"We can't stay here all night," Indy said, trying to sound practical. "What if we're attacked by bandits and tomb robbers? These guys don't work in the daytime, you know. They work at night, and if they find us here, they'll cut off our arms and legs one at a time and make us watch. We're sitting ducks. That's what they'd call us in America, Miss Seymour—"

"Henry," she said sharply. "Listen to me carefully: There is absolutely nothing to be afraid of! You have British blood in you. Try to remember that."

"I'll bet it won't look any different from my American blood when the bandits tear my arms and legs off," Indy said. He always made jokes when he was really scared.

"Oh, do be quiet for a moment, Henry, and let me think." She sat down in the sand with her back against the base of the pyramid.

The wind swirled around them and moaned in Indy's ears.

"Miss Seymour, someone's coming," Indy said, staring hard into the lengthening shadows. His heart started pounding a little faster as he squinted to see who it could be. Tomb robbers? Bandits? "What if it's someone coming to *murder* us?"

Miss Seymour heard the fear in Indy's voice. The next thing he knew she was standing up, putting her arms around him protectively and pulling him close.

"Henry, it's just your imagination. No one is there," she said, trying to sound confident. But Indy felt her hands shaking and knew she was scared, too.

"No, it's not my imagination," Indy said suddenly. Slowly he peeked out from the folds of Miss Seymour's long sleeves. "Miss Seymour, look! It's a guy on a bicycle!"

Chapter 4

Indy and his tutor stood watching a dust cloud blow slowly across the desert. As the cloud came closer, a moving figure could be seen inside it. A lone figure, a man with a scarf wrapped around his head, hiding his face.

"He *is* on a bicycle!" exclaimed Miss Seymour. "How absolutely astonishing!"

The man on the bicycle rode to about twenty feet from them and came to a stop. He dropped his bicycle in the stony sand and stood motionless as the wind whipped his clothes. He wasn't very tall, and didn't look very muscular under his loose-fitting khaki pants and shirt with many pockets. The long white scarf wrapped around his head hid everything but his gray eyes, which, even in the dimming light, were brilliant, piercing, and alert.

As he slowly raised his hands, Miss Seymour straightened even more rigidly, protecting Indy.

"Having a spot of bother?" the man said in a crisp British accent. He reached up and dramatically whipped the scarf from his head.

Indy saw the blond, almost white hair first. Then he saw the handsome thin face of a man about twenty years old.

"Mr. Lawrence!" cried Miss Seymour.

"Hallo, Miss Seymour!" the young man called back. He laughed as if he had just played a successful prank on his teacher.

This was unbelievable. In the middle of the Egyptian desert a man had ridden up on a bicycle, and he knew Miss Seymour!

Miss Seymour cleared her throat as the man came forward. "Mr. Henry Jones, Jr., of Princeton, New Jersey—Mr. T. E. Lawrence, of Jesus College, Oxford. One of the best students I ever tutored. I fully expect Mr. Lawrence to become a leader among men one day."

"How do you do, sir," said Indy.

"Awfully well, as a rule, thank you," said the

young man with a quick lift of his eyebrows. "And please call me Ned. I say! You're not related to Professor Henry Jones, by any chance?"

"He's my father," Indy said.

"Lucky chap!" said Ned Lawrence. "I've read his books. They're brilliant. And now Miss Seymour's tutoring you?"

Indy nodded with some reluctance.

"You *are* a lucky chap!" said Ned, slapping Indy on the back.

Indy was about to disagree vigorously, but something stopped him. Could this man be right?

"What in heaven's name are you doing here?" Miss Seymour asked.

Lawrence smiled and brushed sand from his clothes. "I've been up in Syria, Miss Seymour, looking at the Crusader castles. Fascinating stuff, that! And I thought I'd take in a bit of Egypt before going home." He looked around, as if taking in a bit of Egypt right then and there. Then suddenly he seemed to realize that Indy and Miss Seymour were standing all alone: no guide, no camels. Stranded. "What happened to you two?"

This ought to be good, Indy said to himself.

"We had a slight altercation with our guide," Miss Seymour said.

36

"He ran off with our camels," Indy translated.

"Yes, they do that sometimes," Lawrence said, grinning slightly. "Not to worry. There'll be plenty of camels here by morning."

"But whatever shall we do?" Miss Seymour cried.

"What—*now*, do you mean?" Ned asked.

"Yes!" Miss Seymour demanded, looking positively overwrought.

"Well, let's see," Ned said, looking around. "I'd say . . . gather up camel dung for a fire, and make jolly sure we don't catch cold!"

Fine, Indy thought, except for one thing. What are we going to eat? *Sand*wiches?

They spread out to pick up chips of dried dung. The easy-to-burn fuel lay all over. They also found some small chunks of palm bark and scrub brush that had blown far across the sands from the Nile valley.

What an adventure, Indy thought as they looked for fuel. Sleeping at the pyramids! Indy decided that he'd never met anyone as exciting as Ned Lawrence.

A little later Indy, Miss Seymour, and Ned sat huddled by a small campfire. Indy watched the shadows of flames flicker on Ned's face. Even though it was close to midnight Indy was wide awake, listening to every word this amazing man spoke. Indy was certain that the stars that speckled the desert's black sky were listening, too, hypnotized by Ned's voice as he told stories about the tombs of the pharaohs.

"Inside a pyramid, time stands still," Ned said, poking the fire with a stick. "It has no meaning. When you open a tomb, you let in the light—the first light that place has seen for three or four thousand years. Your feet are the first to tread that floor since the feet of the men who made it and sealed their dead king into it. You may even see their footprints going before you in the dust."

"Gosh," Indy said. He closed his eyes and imagined a torchlight procession of Egyptians carrying the wrapped, pungent body of their pharaoh, laying him gently into a coffin, sealing the coffin inside a stone sarcophagus.

"And yet it's like yesterday!" Lawrence went on. "You see a finger mark on a painted surface, a garland of withered flowers dropped along the way. You are breathing the same air as the men who laid the mummy to rest. . . ."

"I'd sure like to do all that when I grow up," Indy suddenly said.

Ned smiled. "So you would like to be an archaeologist someday?"

"Sure, if that's what you call the person that does all that stuff—digging up ancient people and buried treasure and everything."

"It requires a *great deal* of study, you know," said Miss Seymour. She sat opposite Indy with her back against the base of the pyramid. Her eyelids drooped with sleepiness. In fact, until she spoke, Indy had thought she *was* asleep.

"Henry's not afraid of study, I'm sure," said Ned. "Maybe one day he'll even add a new page to history or discover a treasure beyond price."

"And get rich," Indy said.

"No, Henry," Ned said. "Archaeologists don't get rich. Not in the way you mean. An archaeologist doesn't steal from the past for his own gain. He opens the past, so that everyone may learn from its treasures."

The fire snapped unexpectedly, sending small bits of flame skyrocketing into the air.

"What's it like inside a tomb?" Indy asked. "Why did they have all the furniture and plates and bowls and jewelry in there with them? They didn't *really* need that stuff. They were dead!"

"Yes," Ned said. "But the Egyptians believed that the spirit would remain in the tomb and would need food, clothing, and shelter, just as we do."

"Really?"

"Really."

"Is it true?"

"No, Henry," Miss Seymour put in. "It is not true. But it *is* what the ancient Egyptians believed."

Indy was silent for several minutes. He watched the flames of the fire and imagined the spirit of a mummy rising from its coffin and wandering around in the tomb.

"What *does* happen when you die?" he finally asked, fully expecting Ned to have the answer.

"You know very well," Miss Seymour said.

"You mean, if you're good your soul goes to heaven with the angels and stuff?" Indy said, repeating what his mother had told him.

"That's what Christians believe," Ned said, stretching out on his back to watch the stars. "Other people have different answers."

"Like what?"

Ned sat up with a jerk, as if he had been hoping Indy would ask that very question. "Well, I'll tell you. A good Moslem, when he dies, will go to paradise, which, according to the Prophet Mohammed, is a delightful place, especially if you're a man. A Hindu, however—well, he believes in reincarnation."

"What's that?"

"It means that when the body dies, the soul just reappears in another body and lives again. And it moves on again and again."

"The same soul?"

"Yes," Ned said.

"But in different bodies?" Indy asked.

"Yes. To the Hindu, all life is sacred, from the meanest living creature to the most holy man," Ned replied. He sat back and looked up toward the night sky, then back at Indy. "Where do we come from? Where do we go? It's one of the truly great mysteries—and the spark of most great religions. That's why nearly all of them have an answer to what happens when we die."

Indy's head was practically spinning with ideas. Heaven. Paradise. Reincarnation. "But which one is true?" he finally asked.

Ned laughed and rubbed his hands through the sand. "No one has come back to tell us. But Henry, if you should meet a mummy one night, you can always ask him."

"Did you say *meet* a mummy and *ask* him?" Indy asked, his throat tightening.

"Yes, Henry," Ned said, lowering his voice to a near whisper. "When a mummy's spirit returns at sunset and enters his miserable shriveled body, he rises slo-o-owly from his dusty

coffin and cree-ee-ps out into the darkness . . ."
Ned stood up, very slowly, and walked toward
Indy. Just then a jackal howled hungrily in the
distance.

"And," Ned continued, "if you should chance
to hear the shuffle of his bony feet on the sand—
shuffle-shuffle, shuffle-shuffle . . ." He was only
a few feet from Indy, standing over him with
his arms raised. "If you should meet this
mummy gliding across the desert sand, it may
well be he will answer your questions, Henry—
but only if you return with him to his tomb."

Indy tried to speak but his tongue was frozen. Mummies coming back to life! What a
wonderful, terrible idea!

"Mr. Lawrence, please!" Miss Seymour re-
proached him. "Kindly refrain from filling the
boy's mind with superstitions."

"Is it only superstition?" Indy asked breath-
lessly.

Ned lay back down on the sand. "I dare not
say," he said mysteriously. "But how would you
like to find out for yourself?"

"What do you mean?" Indy asked.

"I'm going upriver Monday, to a spot near the
Valley of the Kings. A friend of mine is work-
ing on a dig with Howard Carter. Carter's a
brilliant archaeologist. We may discover a

tomb—and you could lead the way into it, young Henry. What would you say to that? Want to come?"

Indy's imagination was having a field day already, picturing the pitch-black entrance to a tomb, the dusty sarcophagus in a torchlit chamber, the feeling of ancient eyes watching his every move.

"Can we, Miss Seymour?" Indy pleaded.

"May we," she corrected him sternly.

"May we? May we go?"

Miss Seymour shook her head uncertainly. "Your father will have to give his permission."

"He will!" Indy cried out. "I know he will—as long as we don't tell him we were out all night at the Great Pyramid."

"We shall have to tell him—if he asks," Miss Seymour said, with a worried look on her brow.

"Yes," Indy said. "But he won't ask . . . will he? I mean, he and Mother are away from Cairo. They don't even know we're gone."

"I don't suppose they do," Miss Seymour agreed. Then she was quiet, thinking for a moment. "Perhaps it is best if we never say a word about this episode, Mr. Jones." She gave him a quick, private smile.

"I won't talk if you won't," Indy promised, beaming.

Chapter 5

"Henry, I've missed you so," Indy's mother said as she entered the hotel suite late the next day. She wrapped her arms around him. "Did you miss us while we were away?"

Indy hugged his mother in return—and when he did, sand dropped onto the carpet from all the folds and creases of his clothes. "Uh, the truth is, Mother, Miss Seymour and I have been so busy I almost didn't remember you were gone," Indy said. "You'd be surprised how exciting sight-seeing can be around here."

Then he broke away and made a bee-line for

his father, who had already seated himself at the small writing desk. "Father, may I please go to the Valley of the Kings?"

"To *where?*" Professor Jones said, looking up with interest.

"The Valley of the Kings," Indy repeated. "You see, we went to the Great Pyramid yesterday, and the most amazing man I've ever met rode up on his bicycle. His name is Ned Lawrence and he used to be a student of Miss Seymour's. He knows everything about archaeology and living in the desert. He said he would take me and Miss Seymour to the Valley of the Kings to see a real archaeological dig. And we get to meet Howard Carter and maybe even discover a real mummy!"

"Henry . . . ," his mother started to say in a reproving tone.

But Professor Jones interrupted her. "By Jupiter! What a lucky fellow you are, Junior."

"You mean I can go? *May* go?" Indy said.

"Of course you may, Junior," said Professor Jones. "Carter is first-rate. And besides, your mother and I will be busy here at the university. You and Miss Seymour should go."

"Thank you, Father," Indy said. He was almost bursting with excitement.

"And, Junior—here's something I want you

to take on your journey," Professor Jones said. From a desk drawer, he removed a small notebook and held it out to his son.

Indy took the notebook carefully, holding it as if it were a treasure. It was a beautiful object—a blank book with red marbled covers and red leather trim on the corners and spine. Inside, there were many pages of unlined creamy vellum paper. It was very much like the small diary Indy's father always kept, which Indy had seen him write in so many times.

"Everything that you see, smell, taste, or think may be important to you one day," his father told him. "Write down anything that interests you or strikes you. Start your journal."

"Thank you. I will," Indy said softly.

He headed for the door. "And don't neglect your studies, Junior," Professor Jones called after him.

"No, sir," Indy said seriously.

Indy waited until he was outside in the hall. Then he shouted, "Yippee!"

He dashed down the hall to Miss Seymour's hotel room and knocked on her door. It seemed like an eternity before she finally said, "Enter."

"Miss Seymour," Indy gasped excitedly, "my father said we could go!"

For an instant, all too short an instant, Indy

saw her eyes sparkle at the thought of this adventure. Then she returned to her most formal, forbidding tone of voice.

"We must begin packing, Mr. Jones," she said, putting an empty suitcase on her bed.

"Right," Indy said, turning toward the door. But then he stopped. Why did Miss Seymour have to be so stuffy all the time? Why did she have to call him Mr. Jones? It was bad enough that his father called him Junior and his mother called him Henry. Wasn't there anyone who would listen to him?

He turned back toward his tutor. "Uh, Miss Seymour, do you think maybe you could call me Indiana?"

Miss Seymour gave him a puzzled look. "Indiana?" she said.

"I want people to call me Indiana, that's all," Indy said.

"Were you not born in New Jersey?" asked Miss Seymour.

"Yes, ma'am," Indy said.

"Well, I suppose it *would* be awkward calling you New Jersey," she said.

"It's not the state," Indy said. "Indiana is my dog. I really miss him."

Miss Seymour said nothing, which Indy thought was pretty good. At least she wasn't criticizing him. "You *are* a long way from home, aren't you?" she said.

"Yes, ma'am," answered Indy.

Miss Seymour was silent for a long time as she continued to pack. Finally she spoke again.

"I'm afraid I couldn't possibly call you Indiana, Mr. Jones. It would not be . . . dignified. But you have given me food for thought. Now, as you can see, I am almost entirely packed. It's time that you packed too."

Early the next morning Indy and Miss Seymour hurried downstairs to meet Ned, who was waiting with a carriage.

But once Miss Seymour and Indy were seated, Ned remained outside and said a few words to the driver. Then he closed the door behind them.

"Are you not joining us, Mr. Lawrence?" asked Miss Seymour.

Ned gave Indy a wink. "I'll be along jolly quick, I promise."

Then he jumped on his bicycle and took off. An instant later, so did the carriage.

"Must he drive so fast?" Miss Seymour complained.

The carriage was moving at top speed through the streets of Cairo, bouncing her and Indy in their seats like lightweight balls.

"I'll betcha this guy has never been challenged to a race before," Indy answered, holding on for dear life. But every other word was cut off by another jolt from the carriage. "And *never* by someone on a bicycle!"

He craned his neck, trying to see Ned. "He's winning!" Indy cried.

Ned was pedaling like a madman, staying way ahead of the carriage in the race.

When the carriage driver finally halted his tired and confused horse at the Cairo docks, Ned was there already, leaning casually on his bicycle.

"Nothing like a little morning exercise," he called cheerfully, bounding over to open the door for Indy and Miss Seymour.

"Perhaps next time," Miss Seymour said imperiously, *"I'll* take the bicycle."

Ned helped her out of the carriage, laughing and giving Indy a private wink. Then he put a hand on Indy's shoulder.

"Come along. Let's see about tickets for the first steamer boat to Thebes."

"Thebes?" questioned Indy.

"Thebes was the ancient capital of Egypt. Nothing left of it now but ruins of temples and monuments. The town on that site today is called Luxor. From there it's just a short ride to the Valley of the Kings."

"I'll stay with the bags—and your bicycle," Miss Seymour said, sitting down on a trunk and unfolding her parasol for shade.

Ned led the way to the ticketmaster's office, a tiny wooden shack around the corner and near the water, at the edge of the docks.

"Good morning," Ned said to the man behind the counter as he and Indy squeezed in.

The ticketmaster wore a European suit and must have weighed about three hundred pounds. The counter took up most of the room, and the man took up almost all of the space behind the counter.

"What can I do for you?" the ticketmaster asked.

"We'd like to book passage for three on the first steamer to Thebes," Ned said.

"That would be the *Aquard*. Leaves on Thursday."

Thursday? That's three days away, Indy thought. He could see that Ned was thinking the same thing.

"What leaves sooner?" Ned demanded.

"A dhow," said the man, with a laugh. "They leave all the time."

"Passage for three," Ned said, slapping money on the counter.

"Sir, are you aware that most of the 'passengers' on that ship will be chickens and sheep? Do you know what a dhow is?"

Ned took a deep breath and said, "A large sailing vessel with an upswept bow and one tall mast with one very large sail. It is a cargo ship, which was also used, shamefully, during the slave-trading years."

"I see that you do know," the man said. "But are you sure you want to travel with the boy on a ship like that? Thebes is nearly four hundred miles away."

Ned grabbed Indy's shoulder and shook him playfully. "This, sir, is not a boy, but an archaeologist in apprenticeship!" Indy beamed.

"Looks like a boy to me," the man grumbled, handing Ned three passes.

In less than an hour, Indy, Miss Seymour, and Ned were sitting on the crowded deck of the boat. Indy perched on a crate while Ned found a place to stash his bicycle and Miss Seymour took a seat in the bow. Indy watched his tutor open her parasol against the blazing sun. Funny, he thought, she looks just as comfortable here as she did on the ocean liner in the middle of that storm.

Miss Seymour ignored the squawking chickens on board. As the dhow sailed lazily up the Nile River, she opened a book and began to read. But from time to time she looked up and gazed thoughtfully at the lush green band of scenery on both sides of the Nile. Then she checked that Indy was attending to his studies.

Indy tried to concentrate on the history book that lay open on his lap. He was reading about Napoleon, the great French emperor. More than one hundred years ago, while still a general, Napoleon had marched into Egypt and taken over Cairo. He had brought in archaeologists and scholars who revived the study of ancient relics. But Napoleon had been dead eighty-seven years, while the robed women washing clothes along the banks of the Nile, the children swimming naked, and the men fishing were very much alive. And they were wonderful to watch as the dhow sailed past them.

The river was amazing to Indy, so peaceful and gentle in its flow. In some places it was so narrow that the dhow passed close to the banks. Then Indy could see an occasional crocodile sunning itself or the cotton plants growing in the cultivated fields.

Indy even waved to some of the people he saw, and they waved back. Maybe they thought *he* was just as different, just as interesting to watch as they were.

As Indy turned back to his book, he realized

that someone, one of the tall Arab crewmen, was standing very near. Other crewmen had crept up and were watching Indy intently.

Suddenly the man spoke to Indy in Arabic. His voice sounded strange, maybe even angry.

What did he want? What was he saying? Indy didn't understand, and even if he could, he wouldn't be able to answer. Not knowing the man's language made Indy feel frightened and alone.

The man leaned closer to Indy and repeated the words. But Indy was helpless to understand or answer. He sat silently, staring down at his book and wishing the man would go away.

"He wants to know what you're reading," Ned said, coming over to rescue Indy.

Oh, was that all? Indy relaxed a little with Ned near him. "It's a book about Napoleon," he told Ned. *"She* says I have to finish it."

Ned laughed, then turned to the Arab and gazed directly into his eyes.

"Inahu yak'ra 'an hyat al-muharybin al-ak-wiya," Ned said.

Indy stared in amazement, his mouth falling open. Was there anything T. E. Lawrence didn't know? Of course, Indy shouldn't have been surprised that Ned spoke the language so fluently. Ned seemed to love everything about the Arab culture. He even dressed like an Arab a lot of the time.

"I have told him," Ned explained, turning back to Indy, "that you are reading the life of a mighty warrior."

The crewman, now smiling, moved closer to Indy. With one of his large hands he tilted Indy's face up until they were looking in each other's eyes.

"*Qadamah mawthu'a batiyah tarik Allah,*" the man said.

"What did he say?" Indy asked, looking at Ned questioningly out of the corner of his eye.

"He said that your feet are placed on the pathway to God. These are wise people, you see. They value knowledge above all other things."

The dhow crewmen smiled at Indy as if he were a special prize. Indy felt himself blush— both from the attention and also because he was ashamed that he had been afraid.

Once more Lawrence exchanged a few words with the Arab. Then he translated for Indy.

"I said to him, 'Peace be with you, Father.' And he answered, 'And with you, young bright-haired lord.' "

Indy smiled at the Arab. Things sure were easier when you knew what people were saying.

Chapter 6

The dhow sailed on for days, making the four-hundred-mile journey to the Valley of the Kings. Indy grew restless on the cramped boat, tired of his studies and eager to put his feet on solid ground. And he could tell that Ned felt the same way. Every so often, he and Ned exchanged a look that said, "Doesn't this boat go any faster?"

Miss Seymour, however, seemed to be putting up with the journey pretty well. Indy had to admit that she never complained about anything—not the monotony, or the uncomfortable quarters, or the heat.

She almost looks like she's enjoying it! Indy thought.

One afternoon, Indy again heard Ned speaking to the Arabs.

"Where did you learn to speak Arabic?" he asked, impressed.

"I started at home, but I didn't get very far until I came out here," Ned said. He climbed up and sat on the crate next to Indy. "Henry, would you mind if I gave you a bit of advice?"

Indy shook his head quickly. Mind advice from Ned? Was he kidding? Indy wanted to hear *anything* T. E. Lawrence had to say!

"Well, here it is: Wherever you go, Henry—whatever countries you visit—learn the language. It's the key that unlocks everything. It's where you always must start."

Indy nodded, although privately he was wondering how he would ever learn Arabic.

"Have you got that journal your father gave you?" Ned asked.

"Sure. It's in my travel case," Indy said, hopping off the crate and digging around in his bag. He pulled the small book out and held it tightly in his hands.

"Well, here's something you can put in it," Ned said with a twinkle in his eye. "Follow me."

Indy followed Ned to the bow of the boat,

where Miss Seymour was sitting, still engrossed in her own book. Ned unlashed a long leather tube that had been strapped to his other gear. From the tube, he pulled out a scroll of thin papyrus and unrolled it. The paperlike material was covered with hieroglyphs—ancient picture writing. "Have a look at this, Miss Seymour," Ned said.

"That must be thousands of years old!" Miss Seymour said with delight.

"Three thousand, to be precise," said Ned as he gazed at the scroll with reverence.

"What is it? What does it say?" Indy asked.

"It's a description of the funeral ceremonies of a dead king," Ned said. "Fascinating reading—even thirty centuries later."

Indy examined the lines, squiggles, and drawings, which were still bright on the fragile scroll. Fascinating reading? Who could read it? He was better at understanding the dhow crewmen!

"Is it a picture language?" Indy asked.

"Almost. But not exactly," Miss Seymour answered. "Hieroglyphs represent sounds, a little like the letters of our alphabet."

Indy studied the pictures with a look of complete puzzlement on his face. Ned laughed.

"Look: Suppose it were English and I wanted

to write my name," Ned explained. "I might draw a needle—that gives you the 'N.' Then an egg for the 'E'—"

"And a donkey for the 'D'!" Indy chimed in. "N-E-D—Ned!"

"Yes," Ned agreed. "Though I'm not sure I like the 'donkey.' "

It was Indy's turn to laugh.

"Some of the pictures stand for two or even three sounds, and sometimes entire words," Miss Seymour went on, always the teacher. But Indy didn't mind getting a lecture this time. Hieroglyphs were fascinating! Trying to read them was like cracking a secret code.

"Look at this one," Lawrence said. He pointed to a picture that looked something like a sandal strap. "This represents the sound *ankh*, which means 'life' or 'to live.' The *ankh* was a powerful magic symbol for the Egyptians."

"Magic?" Indy asked. This was getting even better!

"Well, it was more like something you could use as a good-luck charm," Miss Seymour said. "And '*ankh*' was often written with two other symbols, which together made up the most famous Egyptian charm."

"Which ones?"

"These," Ned answered. He pointed to a picture that looked something like a hand drill, and told Indy that it was an abbreviation for the word *"wedja,"* meaning prosperity. The third symbol was a folded bolt of cloth. It stood for the "s" in the word *"seneb,"* which meant health.

Indy drew the three drawings himself on the first page of the diary his father had given him. *"Ankh, wedja, seneb.* Life, prosperity, health," Indy said, memorizing the hieroglyphs and translating them at the same time.

ankh
life

wedja
prosperity

seneb
health

"Well played!" Ned said with a smile of approval. "You'll be fluent by the time we arrive at the dig!"

Late that afternoon, when the heat of the day was cruelest, the dhow docked at Thebes. Indy and Miss Seymour got on donkeys while Ned insisted on riding his bicycle. Together they traveled to a harsh, dry, rocky valley not far away. In the background were mountains, just as rocky, just as dry. Nothing seemed to grow here. The land was parched.

The last bit of the road was cut through a mountain pass with huge boulders on the side and gravel on the ground. As they passed through, Ned stretched out a hand to everything that lay below and said, "This is the Valley of the Kings."

For a moment, they stopped their donkeys and looked at the valley before them. Indy knew that the Valley of the Kings was a famous sacred burial ground for many of the pharaohs of ancient Egypt. After years of watching other kings build pyramids as royal tombs, and then finding that the tombs were frequently vandalized and robbed, one pharaoh decided to try something different. King Thutmose I had his tomb built in this valley, far away from the pyramids. Thutmose hoped that if his tomb were well hidden, grave robbers wouldn't be able to find it.

After that, many of the pharaohs who followed him did the same thing. They hid their tombs by digging secret rooms into the sides of the stone cliffs. Then they covered the entrances. All the tombs were in this very same valley. Eventually it became known as the Valley of the Kings.

Non-royal tombs were dug in other valleys

for miles around. And many of these were just waiting to be discovered! Ned led the way around the mountain pass to a smaller valley nearby, where Howard Carter was at work.

Indy looked across the valley in awe. So this was an archaeological dig! It was nothing like what he had expected. Indy thought an archaeological dig meant one or two guys with a shovel. He wasn't prepared to find that Howard Carter's camp was more like a city of its own.

All the sounds of labor collided with each other head-on. Dozens of Egyptian workers were present, some digging into the base of the cliffs and others carrying away the debris. There were horses and wagons pulling, hauling, hurrying. Many Egyptian boys, some no older than Indy, carried water to and fro. And everywhere the mountains echoed with the sounds of the Arabic language.

"How many tombs are there?" Indy wondered out loud. "And are they all filled with treasure?"

"Alas, King Thutmose's plan didn't work," Miss Seymour said. "Even here, the grave robbers had their way. Dozens of tombs have been discovered. But in none have all the treasures been found intact."

"Well," Ned said, "if anyone can find an untouched tomb, believe me, it's Howard Carter. Absolutely brilliant archaeologist. You will soon meet him, Henry. And my friend Rashid."

As Indy and Miss Seymour followed Ned, they walked past the large and small tents that made up Carter's camp. There were a work tent and a mess tent—the largest tents of all—on one side. On the other side of the camp, Indy saw a double row of smaller tents that were used as living quarters for the crew. Dust clouds floated everywhere over the site. As far as Indy could see, there was nothing in the landscape but rubble, sand, and stone, plus a few struggling palm trees.

At last they were met by an unusual Egyptian man in his twenties. Indy thought he was unusual because he was wearing a light-colored European suit instead of the simple, loose, long white clothes the Egyptian workers wore. He seemed happy to see them.

"My dear Ned!" the man called, rushing over to shake Ned's hand nonstop, until Indy wondered if he was trying to yank it off. "How positively delightful to see you." He spoke with an accent that was a combination of British and Arabic.

"May I introduce Miss Helen Seymour and

Mr. Henry Jones, Jr.? This is my good friend, Rashid Sallam," Ned said, still not in possession of his hand.

"Delightful! Delightful!" Rashid said before anyone else could speak. "Welcome to you both. Well, my friend Ned, you are in luck. We have just discovered a new tomb!"

Chapter 7

"A tomb!" The words came bursting out of Indy's mouth so quickly that he startled Ned, Miss Seymour, and Rashid.

"A pharaoh?" Ned asked

"No," Rashid said. "Not a pharaoh, I'm afraid. Still, all tombs are important, as Mr. Carter always says."

"True, very true, my friend," Ned said.

As they talked, Rashid led them to a water bucket, where they could rinse the road dirt from their hands and faces and cool off for a moment. The water evaporated quickly in the hot, dry, windy desert air.

"Will we get to see inside the tomb?" Indy asked.

"If it were up to me, young Mr. Jones," said Rashid, a smile spreading over his face, "I would say yes. Go inside. Lead the way. But it is for Mr. Carter to decide who of us will have the privilege of seeing our long-buried ancestor."

"What do you think my chances are?"

Rashid drew his lips tightly together and shrugged. "You are the first young-person visitor. It is hard to say."

Suddenly shrill whistles sounded an alarm in the distance.

"Don't move!" Rashid said sharply.

An instant later, a loud explosion rocked the ground under Indy. His knees buckled, and for a moment he thought the earth was opening up at his feet. Bits of sand showered down on him.

"Oh, my. What was that?" Miss Seymour said.

"That was Demetrios, our demolitions expert, blowing up a rock to clear the road to the camp," Rashid explained. "He makes the most wondrous loud explosions. But there is no need to be terrified."

"Why, thank you," Miss Seymour said, smiling at his charming manner.

"There he is, over there," Rashid said, pointing to a burly Greek man with smooth olive skin. He was about forty years old and powerfully built. He was holding a detonator box. "Now we must wait for the 'all clear' signal."

Indy watched as Demetrios stood up and fired a flare pistol into the sky. High in the air, the flare burst into a brilliant green.

"Now we are all quite safe," Rashid said, beaming. "You should speak to Demetrios sometime, young Mr. Jones. He has many interesting stories to tell of his life in Greece. Now, excuse me, please." Rashid turned to a small group of workers who were sitting in the shade of a large boulder. One of the Egyptians was dressed like Rashid, but his linen suit was crumpled. On his head sat a small red hat called a tarboosh.

"*Ye,* Bassam! Come here!" Rashid called to the man and then turned back to his visitors. "Bassam Ghaly is the overseer of the workmen. A most untrustworthy sort of chap."

Bassam Ghaly approached reluctantly. "Yes, Mr. Sallam," Ghaly said in a hoarse voice. "What do you want?" Ghaly was in his fifties and looked as solid as the rocks he and his men were digging through.

"Why are those men sitting idle?" Rashid asked.

"They are afraid," Ghaly croaked in his rough voice.

"Afraid? Afraid of what?" Rashid asked.

"They say there is a curse on the tomb."

"A curse?" Indy gasped. "You mean, like a curse to make people die?"

"Shhh," warned Miss Seymour.

"Ridiculous!" Rashid exploded at Ghaly. "You know there is no such thing as a curse!"

"But that is what the men are saying," Ghaly replied, giving Rashid an angry stare.

"Put the men back to work at once," Rashid said. "At once, Mr. Ghaly."

He was not loud, but he was firm. If there was going to be trouble, Indy knew it would start now.

Bassam Ghaly wiped his hands against his chest and slowly turned to walk away.

"I don't trust that fellow," Rashid said, lowering his voice. "Sometimes I think he encourages them in their superstitions."

Indy could tell Rashid didn't like Bassam Ghaly very much. And Indy didn't like him very much either. But he was fascinated by the curse.

"There could be a curse, couldn't there?" Indy asked Rashid.

Rashid laughed. "Of course not. These are tales for idle women and little children," he said.

67

Suddenly he remembered who he was talking to. He looked at Miss Seymour and then at Indy and blushed. "Oh, I am so sorry. A thousand pardons, please."

Miss Seymour smiled and said, "There is absolutely nothing to pardon, Mr. Sallam."

"Then let us pay our respects to Mr. Carter," Rashid said, leading the way to the largest of the tents.

Just as they entered, there was a brilliant flash. A cloud of acrid smoke followed the small explosion. For a moment, Indy thought he had been blinded. But then the smoke cleared, and Indy saw a photographer, a man in his thirties with a neatly trimmed little beard. The man wore round wire-rimmed spectacles, and he was holding the flash tray of a large plate camera. The camera was perched on a tripod in front of a long wooden table.

Spread out on the table were Egyptian painted pots, scraps of linen cloth, and earthenware figures. All fragile and old. Ned explained that the objects found at an archaeological dig were always photographed as soon as they were discovered, as a way of keeping records. Sometimes, with very fragile pieces, the photograph was the only record that survived—because the artifacts soon crumbled into a pile of dust.

"Finished, Mr. Carter," said the photographer.

Indy had been so busy looking at the artifacts on the table and listening to Ned that he hadn't noticed there was someone else in the tent. Sitting at the far end was a thin, handsome man with a heavy black mustache. Even in the heat of the day he wore a white linen suit, a vest, and a long-sleeved shirt with an ascot neatly tucked into the open collar.

Rashid made introductions quickly. The man with the ascot was Howard Carter. The photographer was Pierre Duclos. Ned almost forgot to shake hands because he was so engrossed in what he saw on the table. "Remarkable specimens," Ned kept saying.

"We found these last month," said Howard Carter. He was polite but brisk, one of those people who never wanted to waste words or time. "All Eighteenth Dynasty."

"From 1555 to 1335 B.C.," Miss Seymour told Indy in her tutor's voice.

Carter walked to the table and scooped up something. He held out to Indy a small piece of clay with delicate small designs impressed in it. Hieroglyphs.

"It's a seal, young Mr. Jones," Carter said. Enthusiasm crept into his voice. "A royal seal.

It bears the name of a king, Tutankhamen."

"The boy-pharaoh, Mr. Carter?" asked Ned.

Carter nodded. His face showed as much excitement as Ned's. The name of the dead king seemed to charge the air in the tent.

"Boy-pharaoh?" Indy repeated, curious to know everything about him. "How old was he?"

"About eighteen when he died," explained Howard Carter. "And probably not much older than you when he became king. It's a fascinating period."

"Do you think his tomb still exists?" Ned asked.

"I'm certain of it, Mr. Lawrence," Howard Carter replied, fingering the clay seal of the boy-pharaoh in his hand. "I don't know why his seal was found near another person's tomb, but it makes me think that I'm on the right track after all. I'm prepared to spend my life tearing apart these mountains to find Tut's tomb, which we shall, with hard work and a great deal of luck. I have an almost superstitious conviction—not very scientific, I'm afraid."

"What about the tomb you found yesterday, Mr. Carter?" Miss Seymour asked.

"Also Eighteenth Dynasty, but, alas, not the king's." Carter picked up another seal, which was smaller than the boy-pharaoh's. "This tells us his name was Kha. He seems to have been some kind of architect or engineer. We may know more when we open his tomb."

Open his tomb. Ned's words at the campfire in the desert suddenly ran through Indy's mind. "Inside a pyramid, time stands still," Ned had said. Indy wanted to see the new tomb more than anything in the world.

"Will you be the first ones inside?" Indy asked. "I mean, since they put the mummy in?"

"I hope so," answered Howard Carter. "I hope that even though we are entering three thousand years after the burial, for once we will have beaten all the tomb robbers."

"May I come?" Indy asked. He knew it wasn't the most polite thing to blurt out. And he didn't need Miss Seymour shaking her head and *tsk*ing him from the corner of the tent to know it. But he had decided to become an archaeologist, and he wanted to get started right then and there.

"A boy won't be much use," Howard Carter said, without much feeling.

"I'm not afraid of the curse," Indy said, although that wasn't really true. Indy half believed in the curse—and he was a little bit afraid of the whole spooky atmosphere he imagined he'd find in the dark tomb. But he was willing to face anything for a chance to see the mummy.

And he had to say something to make Carter change his mind.

Carter's face looked very disagreeable. "Curse?" he muttered, looking over at Rashid.

Rashid spoke up, shrugging apologetically. "Bassam told them. Talk of the curse is everywhere in the camp."

"How very odd. The man is usually so reliable." Howard Carter turned his gaze back on Indy. Indy felt Carter was looking at him inside and out.

"Forget what you heard, my boy. Tomb curses are pure superstition. There is no ancient Egyptian magic—black or white."

"I know, sir," Indy said. But you're going to have to prove it to me, he thought. Indy carefully picked up another of the clay seals from the table and turned it in his hands to see the hieroglyphs. He recognized the marks—the sandal tie, the hand drill, the folded cloth. *"Ankh, wedja, seneb,"* he said out loud.

Howard Carter's mouth dropped in astonishment. "You can read that?" he asked.

" 'Life, prosperity, health,' " Indy translated.

Slowly Carter smiled and held out his hand for Indy to shake. "By Jove, young Mr. Jones. I was wrong. Accompany us into the tomb—by all means, sir!"

1. Ready to explore the world! Professor Jones, Helen Seymour, Anna Jones, and Indy pose for the camera before embarking on their trip to Egypt.

2. Indy's first camel ride is fun—except for the smell!

3. Arriving at Howard Carter's camp near the Valley of the Kings, Ned Lawrence, Miss Seymour, and Indy are greeted by Rashid Sallam.

4. Rashid orders Bassam
Ghaly, the overseer, to force
his men to resume work
despite their fear of the
mummy's curse.

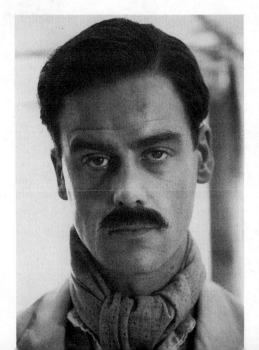

5. At first, Howard Carter is
not thrilled at the idea of Indy
accompanying him into the
newly discovered tomb.

6. Pierre Duclos, Indy, and Miss Seymour dare to enter the tomb—despite the curse over the door!

7. Indy and Miss Seymour run for their lives to escape from poisonous gas in the tomb.

8. Demetrios, the demolition expert *(center)*, and Egyptian workers flee from the tomb site as the news spreads of Rashid's horrible death.

9. Indy meets the mummy!

10. Indy, Ned, Miss Seymour, and Pierre investigate a vital clue in the mystery of Rashid's death.

Chapter 8

"Hieroglyphs!" Indy exclaimed.

Six torches moved in to light up the doorway as Howard Carter studied the symbols painted on the stone above the ancient door.

Carter had kept his promise to bring Indy into the tomb. In single file, Carter, Ned, Rashid, Miss Seymour, Indy, and Pierre Duclos had made their way down steep stone stairs cut into the rock below a cliff. Then they had squeezed through a dark, narrow passage. Bassam Ghaly and his workers had fearfully watched them disappear into the ground. At first, Indy had thought the workers were foolish to be afraid. But now that Carter's group had stopped at the doorway to the tomb, his own heart raced. He wanted to go in, wanted to go back. What did the ancient writing say? he wondered. He held his breath, waiting to hear Carter's translation.

" 'He that,' " Carter said, reading the pictures in halting phrases, " 'enters my tomb . . . I shall . . . burn with my fire.' "

The curse! Indy thought. Ghaly had been right!

Carter barked to Rashid, "Break the seals. Open the door."

Curse or no curse, they were going in—now!

Using a fine chisel, Rashid quickly chipped away at the plaster seals on the door. Then he and Ned slid the bolts away.

"Be prepared to run," Carter said. "The room may be filled with poisonous gas after being closed up for so many years."

Swell, Indy thought. A curse *and* poisonous gas—these Egyptians didn't fool around.

Carter gave a nod and the door opened. The narrow passageway echoed with the scrape and creak of the bolt, which hadn't moved in thousands of years.

Indy held his breath. There was no ball of fire. Just silence. Dead silence.

Carter stepped in first, carrying a lighted candle to test the air. If the candle stayed lit, the air was all right. Indy listened to ten long steps click on the stone floor. Another silence. Indy was surprised at how long Carter could hold his breath. Then came a signal from Carter, and everyone followed.

It was a large room, nothing like the narrow passage that had led into the tomb. The ceiling was high, so high Indy couldn't see it in the blackness.

"Look at this!" Carter said.

"Good lord," said Ned. His voice was unusually quiet.

Indy scrambled over to them and stopped in front of a huge sarcophagus—a stone box six feet long, three feet wide, four feet deep—that sat on the floor.

"Kha's sarcophagus!" Miss Seymour said.

"It looks burned to a crisp," Ned said. Just for a moment his torch swept light across his face and Indy could see that his eyes were wide.

"Everything in the tomb is burned," Carter said, walking around and shining a light on the walls. There was thick black soot everywhere.

"The curse," Indy said quietly.

"Someone has been here before us," Rashid said.

"Tomb robbers?" said Pierre.

"Or the curse," Indy whispered loudly. Miss Seymour shushed him, but Indy thought to himself, it's *got* to be. The hieroglyphs were pretty clear about fire.

"Well, there's only one way to find out if tomb robbers have been here," Carter said. "Give me a hand with the sarcophagus."

Ned, Rashid, Pierre, and Carter each took a corner of the heavy stone lid, while Indy and Miss Seymour held the lights.

"One, two, three!" The men groaned under the weight, just barely managing to lift the lid and set it down on the stone floor.

Indy and Miss Seymour moved in close to get a better look.

Light from Indy's torch shined into the coffin for just an instant before he jumped back. "Is *that* Kha?" Indy asked, edging forward again.

"That is Kha," Carter replied.

"Holy smokes!" Indy exclaimed.

The lower half of the mummy was still wrapped in the dark-stained bandages. But above the waist, the bandages had been removed—as if Kha himself had clawed them off, trying to get free. Where the skin still clung to the bones, it was brown and leatherlike. Kha's eyes were open, looking straight up at Indy. His mouth, with its yellow teeth, was open in a hideous, clenched grin. Completing the horrible picture were the bony hands, their thin brown fingers clawlike, bent and ready to strike out.

"Well, the mummy is still here," Carter said completely calmly. "But it's extraordinary."

Ned looked around the chamber, clearly disturbed. "I don't get it, Carter," he said. "Why are there no artifacts?"

"Perhaps they were stolen," Pierre said.

"I don't think so," Carter said. "The door seals were intact. No—there must be another chamber in the tomb."

As if that had been a signal, Ned, Rashid, and Pierre spread out and began searching the walls of the room.

So this is what it's like to be an archaeologist! Indy thought. He had never had so much fun in his entire life. Sure—it was spooky. Maybe even terrifying. But it was wildly exciting, too. A real-life treasure hunt. Who knew what they would find behind the next wall?

Indy stood very still, careful not to disturb the archaeologists in their work. He only moved his torch to shine it on the walls. The flame lit up a bit of painting.

"Over here!" Ned cried. "Look at this!"

Lawrence held his light very near the wall,

revealing a slim, regular crack. Quickly the other men approached, and Carter ran his fingers along the wall. Tiny bits of plaster fell away.

"It's a door!" Carter cried. "Open it!"

Again Rashid's fine chisel chewed away at the ancient mortar while Indy tried to imagine what would be found behind this secret entry. Kha, hold your fire, thought Indy, remembering the curse. Let this one be the treasure door and not the fire door!

Finally the door was completely revealed. Indy helped open it with a tremendous push.

A blast of hot wind blew past Indy from the opened chamber. The flames of the torches turned from yellow to sickening green.

"Everybody out!" gasped Carter. "The air is poisonous!"

Indy felt Miss Seymour grab his hand and pull him along. He took one gasp of air as they ran out of the coffin chamber, bumping into the stones of the passageway. Indy thought he would burst from holding his breath and trying to run up the steps at the same time. Finally they reached the opening. Fresh air. Daylight.

Indy emerged, gasping. Miss Seymour was right behind him.

Boy, Indy thought, she can run pretty fast, for an old lady.

The workers crowded around, muttering among themselves. Indy saw Bassam Ghaly, the overseer, whispering to several of them off to the side. Then Ghaly and one or two other workers came forward as if they wanted to enter the tomb. But Carter waved them all back.

"No one goes in!" he called, motioning to Rashid. "We'll come back in the morning. The air will be clear by then. Put a guard on tonight, Rashid. Choose someone you can trust."

Rashid glanced in Ghaly's direction for just a moment, then looked away. Indy saw a look of hatred in Ghaly's eyes.

"I'll guard the tomb myself, sir," Rashid offered.

"Good," Carter said.

Then Indy noticed that Carter made a gesture not everyone was supposed to see. He patted his right side, just at his waist. That's where a holster would go, Indy thought. Carter was telling Rashid to wear a gun!

"Can I stand guard with you?" Indy asked, his eyes growing wide with excitement.

"That's very brave of you, but I'll be all right," Rashid answered.

That night Indy couldn't sleep. Maybe it was the hot night. Maybe it was the hyenas in the hills, who barked and howled for hours. And maybe it was the mummy. Indy couldn't get old Kha out of his mind. Every time Indy closed his eyes, he saw the half-unwrapped mummy reaching out to him from his tomb.

Finally Indy got tired of tossing on his cot and got up. He peeked outside his tent. There was lots of activity. Demetrios, the demolitions expert, was standing near the mess tent. He was teaching some Egyptian workers a Greek dance. They seemed to be having a great time, moving around rapidly in a large circle with their hands on each other's shoulders and attempting some fancy footwork.

Other workers were walking around, talking with serious faces, and Indy suspected that he knew what they were saying. They were talking about the curse. "He who enters my tomb, I shall burn with my fire." Indy glanced at the flames of a nearby campfire and shuddered.

Miss Seymour was nowhere in sight, and that was a good sign. Indy made a break for it and sneaked out of his tent.

The moonlight brightened his way as he hurried straight for the cliffs. He could see Rashid standing guard at the head of the steps to the tomb of Kha.

As Indy crept along from tent to tent, trying

not to be noticed, he heard something strange. The horses were neighing nervously, as if something was frightening them. Was someone trying to steal a horse—or make a fast getaway? Indy quickly veered down a dirt path that led toward the horses.

As he got close, he ducked behind a big rock that looked a little like an eagle's head. Egyptian workers, four of them, were standing in the distance whispering. Then one of them began to saddle up horses as fast as he could. He looked around every few seconds to see if he had been spotted.

Suddenly, strong hands grabbed Indy from behind, jerking him into the air. Indy kicked and struggled, but his arms were pinned, and his attacker had one hand clamped over his mouth, while another arm held him around the waist.

The strong hands carried him to the group of four men and dropped him right in the middle.

Indy tried to stay calm. "Nice night for a ride, huh?" he said.

A man who had only one eye looked at Indy and said, "Curse."

"Uh, my mom doesn't let me," Indy said.

"The tomb is cursed," the one-eyed man said. "Everyone who stays will die. We don't want to die."

"Bring him with us or he'll tell the others," said another of the men.

Bring him with them? Indy felt his knees begin to shake. "I can't go. I just remembered Miss Seymour is giving me a French test tomorrow."

They started closing in on him. There were five of them and one of him. They were all six feet tall and he was not even five feet tall. They were strong and desperate and wearing sandals—sandals! That gave Indy an idea.

He waited for the men to come closer. Then he leaped into the air, landing with his shoe heels right on the bare toes of two of them.

"Yee-ow!" they cried, hopping on one foot while holding the other. That gave Indy about a second, and he didn't waste it. He took off at top speed and didn't stop until he was back in his own tent.

Were they coming after him? Indy wondered. He peeked outside. No—those guys were in too much of a hurry to escape the curse. They wouldn't bother chasing him. All Indy saw was Rashid, still standing guard in the moonlight.

Indy thought maybe he should tell Ned or Carter or Miss Seymour about the escaping workers, but suddenly he was too exhausted to move.

"Everyone who stays will die." The words

echoed in Indy's head as he drifted off to sleep.

The next morning he was awakened by the sound of feet hurrying past his tent. When he looked out, Indy saw several workers running toward the tomb. Where was everyone else? Indy wondered. Except for the hurrying workmen, the entire camp was quiet. No—it was more than just quiet. There was a terrible strange silence in the air.

Indy got dressed quickly and followed the path the workers had taken. It led to Carter, Ned, and Miss Seymour, who were standing near the opening to the tomb. A group of Egyptian workers stood silently nearby. Bassam Ghaly was alone, off to one side.

"Why's everyone so quiet?" Indy asked.

Ned looked at Indy, but only for an instant. Then, with a worried expression, he stared back into the tomb. "We can't find Rashid. He wasn't at his post this morning."

"But I saw him last night—in the moonlight," Indy blurted out.

Miss Seymour cast a questioning look in Indy's direction, but said nothing.

"Well, he's gone now," Carter said sharply. His face was pale and his white shirt was soaked with sweat. "We've checked his tent and looked everywhere else. I think it's time we looked in the tomb." He was about to lead the way in when Pierre Duclos's voice surprised them all.

"Bonjour, mes amis!" the photographer called.

Ned and Carter turned as if startled.

"Have you seen Rashid?" Carter asked.

"No. Why? Is he not here?"

Carter answered Pierre's question by simply turning back toward the tomb and giving a nod. Ned grabbed a torch and led the way down the steps, into the opening in the cliffside. Indy had to run to keep up with him. Behind them came Carter, Miss Seymour, and Pierre.

"Rashid?" Ned called. The words crashed off the narrow stone walls, hurting Indy's ears.

When they reached the entrance to the large burial chamber, Ned stopped. He let his light fill the room. It was empty. But beyond, on the far wall, the door to the second chamber stood open.

Pitch-black darkness was all they could see inside.

"Let's go," Lawrence said, crossing the burial chamber cautiously. Everyone followed, passing beside the open sarcophagus single file. *"Mon Dieu!"* Pierre suddenly cried out. He stopped, frozen in his tracks.

Indy turned back and saw Pierre gazing into the stone sarcophagus. So Indy moved closer and peered inside, too. The coffin was completely empty!

Indy gasped. "Holy smokes! The mummy's gone!" he cried out. How? Where? Instinctively, Indy spun around to look behind him. Kha was loose. He could be anywhere! Then Indy lowered his voice and said in dead seriousness, "He climbed out of his coffin and got Rashid."

"Henry," scolded Miss Seymour, "stop that nonsense right now."

It's not nonsense, Indy thought to himself. What does she know? But before he could say anything more, another voice cried out in the tomb. It was Ned, who was kneeling in the doorway to the smaller chamber at the far end of the room.

"Oh, no!"

"What is it?" Indy moved toward him.

"Henry—keep away!" said Ned.

Miss Seymour grabbed at Indy's shoulders, but it was too late. He had already slipped through her hands and gotten close enough to look. There, just inside the next chamber, was the dead body of Rashid—and every inch of him scorched by fire!

Chapter 9

"You shouldn't see this," Miss Seymour said, pulling Indy back, away from the dead body.

She almost sounded as if she were scolding herself instead of him for a change, but it was too late for that. He *was* there and he *had* seen Rashid. Rashid, who had been alive and smiling the night before. How could that be him— that lifeless body on the floor? Indy stared in unbelieving horror at the corpse, praying that it would move.

"Poor Rashid," Carter said. His face was a

mixture of anger and pain. "What a dreadful way to go."

Ned looked up and said, "The fire didn't kill him. There's a head wound—here." He touched the back of his own head gingerly, as if it, too, had been injured.

"Someone attacked him?" Carter asked.

"He didn't even have time to draw his gun," Lawrence said bitterly.

Shuffle-shuffle-shuffle. Indy heard footsteps behind him. Was it the mummy? Was Kha going to attack them too?

Indy's heart skipped a beat.

But it was only the sound of Egyptian workers who had crept inside. When they saw Rashid's dead body, they began crying out in Arabic.

"Everyone out!" Carter ordered, annoyed.

The workers quickly left, still wailing. The Arabic cries grew louder, panicky, and Indy guessed that the other workers, waiting outside, had just learned Rashid's fate. Then the sounds died away as the men fled the site.

Indy and Miss Seymour remained huddled together, unwilling to go any nearer the body . . . unwilling to leave. For once, Indy was glad Miss Seymour was there. Pierre stood off to one side, looking tense and uncomfortable.

Carter stood up from the body and began to pace nervously while Ned examined Rashid further.

"We'll have to take him to the nearest authorities downriver," Carter said. "There's bound to be a police inquiry. I'll go myself, of course. I'm responsible, but I don't know how I'll explain this."

What was Ned doing? Indy wondered. Ned's hands seemed to be moving quickly near the body, brushing something.

"Hallo!" Ned cried out.

"What? Find something?" Carter asked, turning.

What was it? Indy tried to see.

"Some kind of silvery-white powder," Ned said. "His legs are covered with it."

"What can it be?"

"I don't know . . . yet," Ned said. He scraped some into an envelope, which he put in his pants pocket. Then he stood up and removed his jacket.

Indy could see Ned's hands trembling as he covered Rashid's body. Then Ned reached up and wiped at his own eyes.

Carter left Ned alone for a moment. Then he took a torch and stepped into the small chamber that he had opened only the day before. Indy wanted to follow him, but Miss Seymour's hand held him back.

"No one's been in there. Nothing's been touched," Carter reported, coming out. "Not that anything looks worth stealing. Kha was not a noble, so he didn't get the royal treatment. No precious objects—no jewels, no gold." He threw up his hands in frustration.

"There doesn't seem to be any motive," Ned said, his voice cracking slightly.

"Yes, there is," Indy said. " 'He that enters my tomb, I shall burn with my fire.' "

"Oh, Henry." Miss Seymour sighed.

"It's the curse," Indy insisted.

"Miss Seymour," Carter said impatiently, "take him out of here. This is no place for a boy."

Before long Rashid's body was carried from the tomb and strapped to a horse. Then Carter asked a few questions around camp, trying to learn who had last seen Rashid alive. Indy told Carter all about seeing Rashid in the moonlight, after the horses were stolen. But Pierre claimed to have seen and talked with Rashid much later than that. Demetrios, however, contradicted them both. He said he had seen Rashid leave his post very early—just after dinner.

Every one of the workers had a different story to tell—but none of them had any proof. No one really knew who had killed Rashid.

Finally Carter rode off with the body. Of course, when the Egyptian workers saw Rashid's scorched body, more talk of the curse began to spread. The atmosphere was filled with a sense of panic as more and more workers fled. Indy noticed that Bassam Ghaly was the only Egyptian worker who seemed unafraid.

Ned stayed alone in his tent until dinner. When he finally came out, he looked pale and shaken. To Indy, Ned had always appeared to have all the answers. But now he seemed not to have any.

Indy and Miss Seymour ate in relative silence, waiting for Ned to speak.

"He was a splendid fellow," he finally said to Miss Seymour. "So young, full of life. Taught me a lot about living here, among his people."

"It's hard to lose people," Miss Seymour said.

For the first time, she seemed to Indy to be saying something that she *knew* instead of something she had *read*. It made her look very different.

Ned balled his hands into fists, but seemed to realize there was no one to fight, so he relaxed them again. "I can't see any reason for it.

I've been over everything a million times. There's no motive." He stared off into the distance for a moment and Indy was quiet. "God! It seems so pointless!"

Around them in the mess tent, there was murmuring from the tables where the remaining workers ate. Demetrios sat on one side with some other people Indy didn't recognize. Pierre was eating only a small piece of bread and talking quietly with some of Carter's assistants. Bassam Ghaly ate alone, looking at no one, at a table at the far end of the tent.

"He was my friend and I shall miss him dreadfully," Ned said.

"But you'll see him again, won't you?"

Ned looked as if he thought Indy was making a tasteless joke. "See him again?"

"In heaven after *you* die," Indy said.

"Rashid was a Moslem, Henry." Ned smiled wryly.

"Okay. He's in paradise, then," Indy said. "You'll see each other there . . . if heaven and paradise are the same place."

"You don't give up on questions, do you, Henry?" Miss Seymour said.

"Not till I get them answered," Indy said.

Ned brushed his hair back. "Rashid is in paradise, Henry. He most certainly is."

"If Kha let him go," Indy added.

"Let him go?"

"The way I see it, Kha rose from his coffin and killed Rashid."

"Henry, listen," Ned said. He slid the kerosene lantern on the table out of the way so they could look at each other. "When I told you those things—about mummies coming alive and walking the earth—I'm afraid I . . . well, I may have . . ."

"Lied?" Indy said calmly, looking down at the table.

"Exaggerated. The truth is, I can't seem to help it. It's . . . something I do."

Ned spoke quietly, as if he were telling secrets he had never told before. Miss Seymour's face grew serious.

"I'm not sure why," Ned continued. "But I often . . . tell stories. You know—make things up. To make them seem more exciting. To make *life*—I don't know—more worthwhile. I dare say I'll probably live to regret it someday."

Indy smiled and looked up. He understood completely.

"So okay, mummies don't walk," Indy said. "That's all right. But something killed Rashid. Can't we find out what?"

They finished their dinner in silence, remembering Rashid. They all knew that until his murder was explained, they could not sleep at night entirely safe.

Early the next morning, three lights glowed dimly through the narrow passageway into the tomb of Kha.

"We shouldn't be doing this," Miss Seymour said, worried.

"Because Mr. Carter isn't here?" Indy asked.

"No, because it's giving my heart nervous palpitations," Miss Seymour said.

"Don't worry. We won't disturb any of the artifacts," Ned said. His positive, energetic self had returned sometime during the night. Now, at the crack of dawn, he was determined to solve the mystery of Rashid's death. "We've got to find out for certain whether anything was stolen," Ned went on. "If so, then we'll have a motive for murder."

As soon as they entered the burial chamber, Indy rushed to the lone coffin, expecting to find it still empty.

"Aaahhh!" he screamed as a hairy black spider scuttled toward his hand.

Miss Seymour grabbed him protectively, but Indy pulled away. I'm okay now, he thought. I just wasn't expecting anything to *move*.

But except for the spider, the coffin was empty—the mummy was still gone. Indy didn't know which was worse: seeing the hideous mummy in the coffin yesterday—or knowing it was hiding somewhere in the tomb today! He hurried to catch up with Ned, who had gone ahead into the small chamber.

It was Indy's first look into the smaller room, and it was a surprise. Everywhere he looked he saw dusty chairs, tables, benches, linen, pottery, boxes, and weapons—all stacked up from floor to ceiling.

Weird, Indy thought. He knew why all those things were in the tomb. These were Kha's possessions—the things the Egyptians believed Kha's spirit would need in the next world. But Indy hadn't expected them to be piled up so carelessly.

Suddenly Indy spotted an unusual shadow on the wall. "What's that?" he cried, pointing.

Ned moved his torch to illuminate a figure in that corner of the room. "I'll be."

It wasn't another body, Indy realized quickly. It was a lifelike, life-sized painted wooden statue of a young man—a bust showing just the head and shoulders. The paint looked fresh and bright. The face was caught in a serious expression, the eyes in a wide-open stare. A band of metal rested on the carved wooden hair of the statue's head.

"This is what Kha must really have looked like," Ned explained.

"He's beautiful," Miss Seymour said.

"He's . . . strange," said Indy.

"He's an important artifact and belongs in a museum. Now keep looking for something that's obviously missing," Ned said. Then he smiled and moved off to read some hieroglyphs on the wall.

Indy stared into the wide-open eyes of the painted wood statue. Why do you look so alive three thousand years later, while Rashid is dead? he wanted to say.

"Listen to this," said Ned, reading the hieroglyphs on the wall. " 'I was beloved of the Pharaoh. May he live, prosper, and be healthy. As a reward for my great service . . . he gave me the precious headpiece . . .' "

"That must be the one the statue is wearing," Miss Seymour said.

Ned finished the hieroglyphs: ". . . with the sacred Jackal with Eyes of Fire."

"Well, this is the headpiece, I guess," Indy said, "but nix on the Jackal with Eyes of Fire. Nothing here but a plain old metal band."

"That would be very unusual," Ned said,

bringing his torch back over. He held it very close to the statue and put his finger on the headband, right in the middle of the forehead. "Hold on. See the two holes in the metal? Something *was* here, but it's been pulled off."

Miss Seymour said the word. "Stolen?"

"Indeed." Ned turned to Indy. "And now we have a motive for the crime!"

Chapter 10

When Indy came out of the tomb, everything was different. Dark clouds strangled the sun. Sand swirled madly in all directions as if the wind wanted to bury the entire camp.

Indy was different, too. He felt uneasy about being alone, and nervous about people standing behind him. Someone had come up behind Rashid, knocked him out, set him on fire. It had happened so quickly he didn't have time to draw his gun, Ned had said.

At dinner that night Indy, Miss Seymour, and Ned huddled together at a long mess table and spoke quietly. They were fearful that if they were overheard, their lives, too, might be in danger. They acted as secretly as conspirators plotting a crime, sometimes speaking only in single words or coded phrases.

"Jackal" was a forbidden word, unspoken but never out of Indy's thoughts.

"The Eyes of Fire?" he asked Ned.

Ned shrugged and drew a small circle, about the size of a cherry pit, in the dust on the mess table. "Precious stones, I should imagine. About this size," he said, rubbing out his drawing quickly.

Indy looked around to see if they were being watched. Some men were eating or drinking water. Again, as on the night before, Bassam Ghaly sat alone. He returned Indy's gaze and quickly looked away.

"What kind of stones? Rubies?" The thought tantalized Indy.

"Or not," Ned said with an embittered laugh. "Perhaps my friend's life was taken for two old stones worth nothing."

"Or maybe the whole jackal was made of gold."

Ned shrugged again. "That would certainly be a motive."

Moving the kerosene lamp near him, Ned took

a scrap of paper from his shirt and quickly drew a sketch of a jackal. Meanwhile, Indy ate hungrily and Miss Seymour brewed a cup of tea.

"The whole thing probably looked like this," Ned said softly, passing the drawing to Indy. It showed an angular jackal's head with ears alert.

Indy looked at the jackal and tried to imagine its shape gleaming in gold.

"I know this much," Ned said. He lowered his voice even more. "No Egyptian would remove the mummy from the coffin. That would be a sacrilege."

"European, then?" Miss Seymour asked.

Ned nodded.

"Well, that's a clue!" Indy said. Now they had a way of separating who *could* from who could *not* have been the murderer. *European.* He counted people on his fingers to see how far the clue would lead them. "Carter," he whispered, raising one finger.

Ned gave him a skeptical look. "Hardly."

Indy put his finger back down and started again. He looked around the tent and raised three fingers. "Us . . ." Then he raised a fourth finger and said "Demetrios . . ." Finally he raised his thumb. "Pierre!"

Ned squirmed on his bench, unconvinced. "There are other possibilities. What about someone with a foot in both worlds?" His eyes moved sideways and seemed to lock on someone. "Someone who knew enough about Egyptian superstitions to plant the idea of a curse to scare the workmen. Someone who needed money and hated Rashid."

That description matched only one man, and Indy wanted to whirl around to face him. But instead, he whispered his name. "Bassam Ghaly. Are you going to arrest him, Ned?"

Miss Seymour sighed. "On what evidence, Mr. Jones? Mr. Ghaly is not presently carrying the jackal. There are no witnesses saying he was in the tomb. In fact, there was no evidence at all that he was ever there. In a civilized legal system *evidence* must precede *accusations*."

"Miss Seymour is right," Ned said.

Indy drummed his fingers on the table. Couldn't she pick another time to be right?

"We need hard evidence. The jackal itself or . . . I'd almost forgotten!" Ned said. "We *have* evidence. We just don't know what it is." He bent down close to the table and blew away the dust to make a clear spot. Then he took an envelope from his pocket and spilled some of its contents, a silvery-white powder, onto the table.

It was the powder Ned had found on Rashid's

scorched legs inside the tomb.

Indy stared closely and rubbed a little between his middle finger and thumb.

"It looks like magnesium," Indy said.

Ned pulled at his chin. "Henry, you impress me."

" 'Astonish' is more appropriate," said Miss Seymour.

Indy beamed. Why bother telling them that the only reason he knew was because a scientist friend of his father's had used some magnesium to do a magic trick once, back home in New Jersey?

"It could be magnesium," Ned said. "And there's one way to find out." Ned struck a match, letting the blue of the flame touch the powder. It made a quiet sizzle, and then a small but brilliant flash of white light exploded.

"Photographer's flash powder!" Ned said, forcing himself to whisper.

"Pierre," Indy said. Unable to stop himself, he turned and looked at the photographer. Pierre sat by himself. He was drinking a cup of tea and wiping his narrow mustache clean after each sip. Nothing he did seemed innocent to Indy now.

"What are we going to do about him?"

Ned laughed. "Five minutes ago you were

asking the same thing about Bassam Ghaly, old chap," he said. "Let's sleep on it for now."

Indy was sleeping in his tent when footsteps outside woke him. It was barely dawn, so he rolled over to sleep some more.

As soon as he did, a hand, smooth yet strong, clamped over his mouth. Indy's body stiffened with surprise. He twisted around and looked straight into the piercing eyes of Ned, who was standing over the cot.

"Sorry," he whispered, "but I had to be certain you didn't make a sound."

The smooth, strong hand relaxed, and Indy drew a deep, uncomfortable breath.

"I need your help, old lad," said Ned.

"Sure," Indy said, sitting up. "With what?"

Ned smiled, but then paused. Indy could tell that Ned had something dangerous in mind. "I'm going to search Pierre's tent."

Indy sat up straighter. Great! he thought. Now things were getting *really* good.

"I thought I'd slip in right now while he's in the mess tent," Ned went on. "So I want you to keep your eyes skinned. If he moves, come quick and tell me."

"What if he catches you, Ned? He *murdered* Rashid. He'll kill you, too!"

"I can take care of myself if I have to," Ned said, lifting his desert jacket and revealing a Mauser pistol tucked in his pants. "But I don't want to have to use it. So play up, old chap. And play the game." Quickly he moved toward the tent opening.

"Trust me, Ned. And be careful."

Ned wheeled around, startling Indy. "Take that back, Henry," he said sharply. Then his voice softened. "That was the last thing I ever told Rashid, and it didn't do him any good."

Then with a nod, Ned was off. Indy watched him make his way down the rows of white tents, until he stopped at one, looked around in every direction, and ducked inside.

Find something, Indy thought, crossing his fingers. But find it fast and get out! Then he remembered: He wasn't supposed to be watching Ned. He was supposed to be watching Pierre! He quickly jumped into some clothes and slipped across camp toward the mess tent.

Don't get caught, Indy told himself. Stay down—and stay out of sight.

Indy ducked behind a smaller tent and tried to stay hidden. From there, when he stuck his head out, he had a perfect view into the mess tent. Its flaps were open, and Indy could see the photographer sitting at a table just inside.

Pierre was drinking tea and eating a thick slice of bread with jam. He wiped his mustache clean after every bite. That's good, Indy thought. Just sit there and have your breakfast—and give Ned plenty of time!

But suddenly Pierre looked over in Indy's direction. "Why are you hiding behind that tent, *mon ami?*" he called.

Nuts, Indy thought. He smiled a nervous "good morning" and stepped out. "How did you know I was there?"

"A photographer would be lost without good eyes, no? He must have eyes in the back of his head."

That would have helped Rashid, too, Indy thought bitterly.

"You are early for breakfast."

"I'm not very hungry," Indy said. He came forward and stood across the table from Pierre, staring at his jacket pockets. Indy hoped he'd be lucky enough to see the bulge of a golden jackal.

"Who can blame you, with this food?" Pierre said, dropping his napkin onto the table. "I would kill for a real French bread."

Indy gulped. Golden jackals, ruby eyes, and now French bread. What *else* would this guy kill for?

"Where is your friend Ned?" Pierre asked. "You are with him always, like a shadow."

"I haven't seen him lately," Indy said with a nervous gulp. "But I'll bet he's busy. Real busy."

"Very mysterious, *mon ami*," Pierre said, raising his eyebrows. "I respect a man of secrets and will say no more."

Pierre stood up, smoothing his mustache one last time with the back of his index finger.

"Well, there is much to do. An opportunity such as this comes once in a lifetime, and one must not waste it."

"Where are you going?" Indy asked, almost too quickly.

"To the work tent, *mon ami*. Always my work is calling me."

As Pierre left the tent, Indy could only guess what his crooked smile meant. He waited a few beats, then followed, ducking behind one tent and then another, always trying to stay out of sight.

But Pierre was moving quickly, taking long strides. Indy stayed hidden to make sure he wouldn't get caught. But when he stood up again, he practically walked into Pierre, who had doubled back to surprise him.

"Why are you following me?" This time there was no smile in Pierre's voice or on his face.

"I'm not following you," Indy said. "I'm going this way, too."

Pierre rested his hand on top of Indy's head lightly. "I do not need a new shadow, *mon ami*," he said.

There was no doubt in Indy's mind that Pierre was serious. It would have been easy for him to squeeze Indy's head like an orange. Instead, tightening his fingers just slightly, Pierre moved his hand, making Indy's head nod "yes."

"I'm glad you agree," Pierre said. He released Indy's head with a smile and walked away again.

For a moment Indy just stood there. Was Ned done in Pierre's tent yet? Had he found the jackal? Was he looking for Indy?

Indy didn't have any answers. But one thing was for sure: Pierre had something to hide. Indy could tell . . . in the way Pierre squeezed his head . . . in the furtive look behind Pierre's normally smiling eyes.

There wasn't time to wait for Ned, Indy realized. Pierre was up to something. He was now heading in the opposite direction—straight for the tomb!

Indy ran toward the cliffs, where the tomb of Kha was still mostly buried under the rubble of a thousand ages. The valley was quiet now, since none of the workers would dig there anymore. All that remained were the curse, the scratch marks where the jackal had once been—and a murderer.

Indy paused outside the entrance to the tomb. He took a deep breath for courage, looked around one last time, and then followed Pierre inside.

Chapter 11

Indy stopped just outside the burial chamber and waited for his heart to slow down. Pierre was inside, moving around, muttering to himself in French, sometimes even laughing. A thin wall of stone was all that separated them—and was maybe all that was keeping Indy alive.

Why did I follow him by myself? Indy wondered. But it was too late to worry about that.

What's he doing in there?

Indy took a step forward, a few slow inches out of the shadow's darkness and toward the light coming from the burial chamber. Another step . . . and another. Suddenly the burial chamber lit up, bright white, like the sun on the desert sand. He's unleashed the curse of fire! Indy thought, covering his eyes and retreating until his back pressed flat against the tomb wall.

Keep still, Indy told himself. Don't even breathe too much—and maybe nothing else will happen.

Another explosion of blinding light! It startled Indy again. Recoiling, he tried to press himself into the solid rock at his back.

With a grinding sound, the impossible happened. The stone behind Indy *did* move. It slid open and Indy staggered backward, catching himself at the last second before falling into darkness.

Maybe Pierre didn't hear that, Indy thought. Wished. Prayed.

Until, from inside the chamber, he heard the unmistakable sound of footsteps, the scratch of leather on the stone floor. It was getting louder, coming closer. Now there was no choice but to back up farther into the darkness, to move as far away from the footsteps as possible. Not that it would do any good. Indy knew he was trapped.

A thin shaft of dim light flowed from the chamber.

He took a step back, and something thin and sharp poked him hard in the back. He froze. What was it?

Indy turned around and came face to face with the mummy!

"Aaaaaiiii!" Indy screamed, twisting to escape.

Its thin bony hand with brown patches of skin touched his shoulder, his face, and then seemed to grab him around the waist.

Run! Get out of here! Indy screamed in his mind. But somehow the weight of the mummy was on him. His feet slipped, and he fell to the floor with the mummy on top of him, staring down. Indy was inches from eyeless sockets, crooked teeth, leatherlike skin, a lipless face pressed tight against his own!

Indy jerked his head away. But his heart didn't stop pounding when he saw another face, alive and coldly staring down at him. It was Pierre! He was holding a torch and looking angry enough to kill.

"No!" Indy screamed. "Don't kill me! Don't kill me like you killed Rashid!"

Suddenly a figure in khaki came down the passageway and in a fury grabbed Pierre, driving him back into the burial chamber. There was a moment of shouting and wrestling, and then

Indy caught a glimpse of Ned. As the world spun dizzily, Indy scampered away from the foul-smelling mummy.

For another moment, Pierre and Ned struggled with each other. But then Indy heard a loud click—the sound of a gun hammer being cocked! Ned had forced Pierre up against a wall and had one hand around his throat. Ned's other hand held his revolver—an inch away from Pierre's nose.

"Are you crazy?" Pierre shouted. "I didn't kill Rashid!"

Ned relaxed his choke hold slightly but kept the gun in place. "Then what are you doing here?" he demanded.

Pierre nodded toward his camera and his flash tray, which were set up by the mummy's coffin. "I was . . . taking some photographs," he said reluctantly. "To sell to the newspapers. There is much money to be made from such a story. . . . A man must live."

Ned backed off, his gun still drawn. Pierre held very still.

"There was magnesium powder on Rashid's body," Ned said. He was stating a fact, but it still sounded like an accusation. Pierre did not mistake it for anything else.

Across Pierre's face came an expression of

understanding. "But I am not the only one in the camp who uses magnesium powder!"

Not the only one? Indy stepped back, and his foot accidentally kicked the mummy sprawled on the floor. There was an unexpected, strange clunking sound. "Look!" he shouted, bending down to pick something up. "This just fell out of the mummy's wrappings."

It was a heavy T-shaped piece of metal with a fat round wooden handle. One end of the handle was stained unevenly—a dark red-brown.

"That could be blood," Indy said.

Pierre took the handle from Indy and turned it in his hands. "It's a dynamite plunger," he said.

Ned said only one word, shouting it as he raced for the entrance to the tomb. The word echoed through the stone hallway.

"Demetrios!"

The demolitions expert? No! Indy thought. Not the man who so happily taught Greek dances to the Egyptian workers. Indy was astonished that Demetrios could be so different in his heart from what he seemed on the outside.

With Ned leading the way, they ran from the tomb and swept into Demetrios's tent. Ned's gun was drawn and cocked. Indy and Pierre followed close behind, and a moment later Miss Seymour appeared.

"Have you found something?" she asked, seeing their excitement.

"I think so," Indy replied.

Inside the tent, everything was neat and orderly. On one side were boxes of equipment, spools of wire, glass jars of chemicals. On the other side, a cot and nothing else.

Indy picked up a jar with a familiar silvery-white powder in it. "Magnesium powder," he said. "For making flares."

Just then Ned found a detonator box under the cot. It had no handle. Ned picked up the T-shaped bar Indy had found in the tomb—the one they all knew was the murder weapon—and inserted it into the box. It fit perfectly.

"But where's Demetrios?" Indy asked.

"His clothes are gone," Miss Seymour said as she pulled a makeshift curtain aside.

"He will be in Port Said by now," Pierre said sadly. "Ready to board a ship."

"Not if I have anything to do with it!" Ned nearly yelled. He threw the detonator on the ground and ran from the tent.

"What are you going to do?" Indy asked, but Ned passed him too quickly to hear. By the time Indy caught up, Ned was astride his bicycle, his revolver and a canteen around his waist. "But . . ."

"Wonderful meeting you, Henry. You're really a splendid chap!" Ned said, already pedaling.

"Ned—don't go!"

"Must, old chap. Rashid's murderer cannot go free. And the jackal belongs in a museum. I've got to make sure it gets there, right?"

Ned smiled but didn't wait for an answer. In his mind there was no choice. Indy understood this much better than he understood why his lower lip had started to tremble. "Ned," he called, running to keep up. *"Ankh, wedja, seneb."*

Ned's brilliant eyes flashed pride and confidence in Indy. He slowed a bit. "I'll write to you. Promise!" he said. Then he began pedaling again like a madman, like a desert sandstorm, the same way he had come into Indy's life. " 'Bye! Don't forget me!" he called, turning his head without slowing his pumping legs.

" 'Don't forget me' . . . as if I ever could," Indy said to Miss Seymour, who had walked up and gently put her arm around his shoulders. "He won't be back, will he?"

"In my experience, Mr. Lawrence is not a young man who retraces his steps," said Miss Seymour. "He only continues straight ahead."

Well, Indy thought sadly as he watched the sand cloud of T. E. Lawrence pedaling toward the horizon, we sure had fun together. Smashing good times, as Ned would say.

They had sat at the base of a gray pyramid at midnight, entered an unexplored tomb, faced a mummy's curse, and solved a murder mystery together. That was quite a lot.

"You know, Mr. Jones, sometimes Mr. Lawrence used to say that meeting me changed his life," Miss Seymour said, and her voice grew soft as she spoke. "I regret that I never told him that he changed mine, too."

"I feel the same way about him," said Indy. "And I'm going to tell him, next time I see him."

"Good for you, Mr. Jones," said Miss Seymour with an approving nod. And then she added, "In years to come, I wonder what I shall think of you?"

"Oh, I bet I'll change your life, too, Miss Seymour," said Indy with a teasing smile.

"We'll see," she said. "For the moment, I know my nerves will never be the same." Then, much to Indy's surprise, she returned his smile. "Now to prepare for our long journey to Cairo, Mr. Jones. But don't worry. I have your studies all planned out."

Indy kicked at the sand. "I'm sure you do," he groaned.

It would be days before Indy found out that Ned arrived in Port Said too late to catch Demetrios, who had sailed on a ship bound for Greece. And it would be a long time before he ever heard of T. E. Lawrence again.

But right then and there—in the Valley of the Kings, in Egypt in May of 1908—young Indiana Jones made himself a promise. Someday he and Demetrios would cross paths again, and he would recover the Jackal with Eyes of Fire.

"Someday I'll get you, Demetrios," Indiana Jones said out loud. "And *then* you'll pay for what you did!"

Historical Note

Howard Carter was one of the most famous archaeologists ever to search for undiscovered treasure or tombs in the Valley of the Kings. For many years, this Englishman excavated in and around the valley, believing all the while that he would eventually find the tomb of Tutankhamen, the boy-king.

Then, in 1922, Howard Carter's dream came true. He found King Tut's tomb—filled with more treasures than any other tomb ever discovered, before or since. Ancient tomb robbers had barely penetrated it, so most of the treasures were untouched. Golden coffins, thrones, jewelry, furniture, statues, alabaster carvings, chests, the mummy of King Tut, and more were all found within.

As soon as the tomb was discovered, however, rumors of a curse began to circulate. Some people believed that anyone who violated a pharaoh's tomb was destined to die an early death. Then, just a few months after the tomb was uncovered and before the treasures were removed, Carter's patron died quite suddenly. This was Lord Carnarvon, the man who had sponsored Carter's work for years and paid for the excavation of King Tut's tomb. Was the curse coming true? Some people thought so. But those who believed in the curse waited to see what fate would befall Howard Carter himself. Carter, however, lived a long and full life, proving once and for all that "the mummy's curse" was merely superstition.

T. E. (Thomas Edward) Lawrence was a real person who loved archaeology as a young man. He also loved the desert, and at the age of twenty-two he toured Syria—on foot! For four years, he lived among Arabs, learning their language and developing a deep affection for their culture.

So it is not surprising that a few years later,

during World War I, Lawrence became a folk hero to the Arab people and a national hero in his native Britain. In fact, he captured the imagination of the whole world. How? By masterminding an Arab revolt in the desert.

Lawrence's rise to fame began when he was assigned as a British Army officer to Egypt. His superior officers knew that he had an extraordinary knowledge of neighboring Arabia (a huge area now divided into Saudi Arabia, Iraq, Jordan, Syria, and other countries). Arabia was under the control of Turkey at that time. The British were fighting the Turks, since the Turks were allies of Germany, Great Britain's chief enemy in World War I. So Lawrence was sent into Arabia to persuade the Arabs there to rebel against the Turks.

Lawrence's job was not an easy one. That was because the Arabs were not one united people. They belonged to many different tribes, who often mistrusted or even hated one another.

Somehow, through his amazing leadership ability and the force of his personality, Lawrence was able to win the Arabs' trust. Then he organized them into an army and taught them how to fight a brilliant guerrilla war—attacking the Turkish railroads, demolishing their bridges, and capturing many Turkish-held towns.

For his efforts, Lawrence became a legend in his own time—known throughout the world as "Lawrence of Arabia."

And what of Indiana Jones? It is unclear from the data on Indy whether or not he ever met either Lawrence or Carter again. (For that matter, it is uncertain whether the real T. E. Lawrence and Howard Carter ever actually knew each other.) But it is known that years later Indy caught up with the villain Demetrios . . . and that he did recover the Jackal with the Eyes of Fire. That, however, is another story—to be told another day.

TO FIND OUT MORE . . .

Ancient Egypt (Eyewitness Books) by George Hart. Published by Alfred A. Knopf, 1990. Shows life in ancient Egypt through hundreds of wonderful full-color photographs and detailed captions. Mummy cases, statues, gold amulets, and other ancient artifacts in splendid detail.

Exploring the Past: Ancient Egypt by George Hart. Published by Gulliver/Harcourt Brace Jovanovich, 1989. An account of ancient Egyptian religious beliefs, hieroglyphic writing, home life, preparation of mummies, and more. Lots of full-color pictures, a map, and a time line.

Egypt . . . in Pictures by Stephen C. Feinstein. Published by Lerner Publications, 1988. See the Egypt that Indy saw, as well as the Egypt of today. Lively photographs of people and places, plus maps and charts.

Tales Mummies Tell by Patricia Lauber. Published by Thomas Y. Crowell, 1985. What natural and man-made mummies throughout the world reveal about prehistoric life and ancient civilizations. Includes the evolution of mummy making in Egypt. Black-and-white photographs show all kinds of mummies in sometimes gruesome, sometimes beautiful, detail.

Mummies Made in Egypt by Aliki. Published by HarperCollins, 1979. Step-by-step color illustrations, adapted from paintings and sculptures found in Egyptian tombs, explain the 70-day process of mummification. Accompanied by an easy-to-read text.

The Riddle of the Rosetta Stone: Key to Ancient Egypt by James Cross Giblin. Published by HarperCollins, 1990. Found in 1799, the Rosetta stone is a slab of rock with inscriptions that enabled scholars to decipher Egyptian hieroglyphs. This book gives a brief history of its discovery, with examples showing how the code was cracked. Black-and-white photographs, prints, and drawings.

The Young Scientist Book of Archaeology by Barbara Cork and Struan Reid. Published by Usborne, 1984. Full-color pictures and a brief text focus on treasures, techniques, and great moments in archaeological history. Perfect for would-be archaeologists like Young Indy.

My Friends' Beliefs: A Young Reader's Guide to World Religions by Hiley H. Ward. Published by Walker and Company, 1988. In this fact-packed book, each chapter focuses on a particular religion's history, leaders, and beliefs. Covers religions mentioned in *The Mummy's Curse* and others. Black-and-white photos.

THE LUCASFILM

F·A·N C·L·U·B

There's a world of adventure awaiting you when you join the official Lucasfilm Fan Club!

Go behind-the-scenes on the new television series *The Young Indiana Jones Chronicles* in each issue of the quarterly Lucasfilm Fan Club Magazine. Exclusive Interviews with the cast and crew, exciting full-color photos and more fill every page! In addition, the latest news on the new *Star Wars* movies is found within the pages of the Lucasfilm Fan Club Magazine as well as interviews with actors, directors, producers, etc. from past Lucasfilm productions, special articles and photos on the special effects projects at Industrial Light & Magic, the latest in computer entertainment from Lucasfilm Games and More! Plus you'll receive, with each issue, our exclusive Lucasfilm Merchandise catalog filled with all the latest hard-to-find collectibles from *Star Wars* to *The Young Indiana Jones Chronicles* including special offers for fan club members only!

If you love the kind of entertainment only Lucasfilm can create, then The Lucasfilm Fan Club is definitely for YOU! But a one-year subscription to the Lucasfilm Fan Club Magazine is not all you receive! Join now and we'll have delivered right to your front door our brand new, exclusive *Young Indiana Jones Chronicles* Membership Kit which includes:

- Full-color poster of 16 year-old Indy, Sean Patrick Flanery!
- Full-color poster of 9 year-old Indy, Corey Carrier!
- *Young Indiana Jones Chronicles* Sticker!
- *Young Indiana Jones Chronicles* Patch!
- Welcome Letter from George Lucas!
- Lucasfilm Fan Club Membership Card

Don't miss this opportunity to be a part of the adventure and excitement that Lucasfilm creates! Join The Lucasfilm Fan Club today!

JOIN FOR ONLY $9.95